D0366795

ASK ME AGAIN

Kindle Edition

Written by Theresa Hodge

For Denise, my beloved sister. Save a place for me in heaven.

Prologue

Death has a way of bringing people back to where they said they would never go. I couldn't believe it had been twelve years since I set foot in that small town in Alabama. Denise and I were best friends ever since we could walk. Even though I hadn't seen her in years, we stayed in touch via email and phone. In all that time, she didn't let me know she was terminally ill. If I'd known, I would have been there for her, no matter what. Two days ago, after learning she died from breast cancer, I hopped on the first thing smoking out of JFK in New York.

After landing at Hartsfield-Jackson airport in Atlanta, I rented a car and drove to Auburn, Alabama where I would be staying at the Hilton in Auburn. I wanted to get checked in and freshened up before heading over to see Weston, who was Denise's husband and also a good friend of mine. They had two daughters and my heart was just broken for their devastating loss. I wished I hadn't stayed away so long. I should have been there for her. All of the should-have, could-have, and would-have emotions ran through me.

Reaching my destination, I parked and grabbed my piece of luggage and shoulder bag. Thankfully, I had registered online, so all I had to do was go to the front desk to retrieve my passkey. Rejecting the offer of help from the bellhop, I made my way over to the bank of elevators that would carry me to my room on the third floor.

Once I found my room, I inserted the electronic key and let myself in. The shower was my first destination. The warm water was somewhat refreshing. Exiting the shower, I opened my luggage and took out a fresh pair of matching undies, a pair of faded jeans, and my favorite Auburn Tigers T-shirt. Sliding my feet into a pair of sandals, I was ready to head out the door. I grabbed my key and purse and the door automatically locked behind me.

As I pulled out of the hotel parking lot, memories of the past assailed me. I thought back to when my mom was alive, and how she used to say, 'Alyssa, if I didn't know any better, I would think you and Denise were conjoined twins.' That was because when we were growing up, you could hardly find one without the other. That was why when Denise started dating Weston Kingsly as a freshman in college, I started dating his best friend about six months later.

When I first met Drake, I was not looking for love. I had my four-year plan laid out in black and white. Ever since I was ten years old, I knew I wanted to be a teacher. And my father expected excellence from me, so I didn't want to let him down. Most of all, I didn't want to let myself down. I didn't want or need any distractions, but life had a way of changing the best laid out plans.

Drake Peterson was six-foot-three inches of chocolate fineness with muscles on top of muscles. He was also the defensive lineman for our Auburn Tigers college football team. Being an honor student, added to his magnetism. Brains and brawn. The two combined turned me on like nothing else.

Denise invited me out for pizza with her and Weston at a little college hangout one night. I should have known it was a setup from the jump, when I saw the extra guy sitting at the table. It was only supposed to be the three of us. Denise waved me over when she spotted me. Drake and Weston stood, when I got to the table. Weston wasted no time introducing us.

"Alyssa this is my boy, Drake. And, Drake this Alyssa, a very good friend of Denise and mine."

I looked at Denise with accusing eyes, as she smiled and twitched in her seat like she was up to something sneaky.

Taking my hand in his, he raised it to his lips. "It's a pleasure to formally meet you, Alyssa. Although I must say, I have already been checking you out around campus."

I jerked my hand from his. I didn't want him to feel my sweaty palms, or know how nervous he was making me feel. It puzzled me that I was so nervous in the first place. Glancing at Denise, I was unsure of what to say as I sat beside Drake in the booth.

"Hi," I responded barely moving my lips.

Denise and Weston started a conversation about how hard Professor Grants' class was that quarter. Eventually, I felt at ease and Drake and I began to make small talk. The more we talked, the more I liked him. I admired that he wasn't conceited or self-absorbed. Before the night was over, he asked me out to the movies and I accepted. Not long after that first date, we were considered a couple on campus. We fell for each other...hard. I made sure I went to all of his home and away games, when I could get there.

The only downside to our relationship was Autumn Blake. She was the dubbed the Campus Queen. The one who could have anyone she chose. She was beautiful – at least on the outside. She had a body any girl would die for and she knew it. She was a Bitch with a capital "B" in all other areas.

Her sights were set on Drake Peterson, and she wanted him with a passion. She didn't even try to hide her desire for him. Meanwhile, Drake swore up and down that he didn't have any interest in her.

I always wondered to myself, how could he not? She was willing to give him what he wasn't getting from me. I came from a real

8

strict home. Mom died when I was only ten years old from cancer. I was an only child, and my dad kept a tight leash on everything I did and everyone I hung out with. I loved my dad more than anything, but I was so glad to have a little freedom in my life when he decided to let me live on campus. That freedom didn't include having sex – until I was married.

Drake promised that he understood and that he loved me enough to wait. He said he knew the first time he met me that he wanted me to be his wife. Looking into his hazel eyes flecked with gold, I believed him. It took everything in me to hold on to my convictions of not becoming sexually active. Even though we did get hot and heavy at times, we never went all the way. I tried to avoid situations of being alone with him.

Finals were coming up, and Denise and I were studying every free moment we had. I saw less of Drake at that point. We had an understanding when it came to test time. We had to make the best grades possible. Drake would be graduating in two weeks and everything depended on his final grades.

After we finished studying that Saturday night, Denise went on her date with Weston. I stayed behind in the dorm studying. Looking around the empty room, I was missing Drake so much that I decided just maybe I would give myself to him as his graduation gift. I made my way across campus to his building and went up the stairs to his room.

Loud music blasted through his door, so I knocked hard so I could be heard over the music. Getting no answer, I was about to leave when I decided to turn the doorknob. Happy the door was unlocked, I walked into the empty setting room. Beer cans were scattered everywhere and there was a dim light coming from Drake's open doorway.

Thinking he was in the shower, I entered his room with plans to strip and surprise him in the shower. On the first three steps into his room, I heard loud moans coming from his bed.

Autumn Blake's ass rose and fell on Drake as if her life depended on it. Drake's big hands were splayed across her behind urging her on. There was no wondering why he wasn't pressuring me for sex. He was getting from Autumn.

Tears streamed down my face. Covering my mouth to stop the loud gasp from coming out, I tried to leave without being seen. But, as I backed out of the room, I knocked over a picture on his desk. A picture that we had taken not too long ago. In the picture, he was standing behind me and I was encircled in the same arms he now had around Autumn.

Hearing the picture crash to the floor, Drake and Autumn turned toward the doorway. Drake looked both confused and shocked to see me standing there. Autumn, on the other hand, had a trumpet smile and gleam in her evil eyes. He pushed her off him so hard that she almost landed on the floor.

I turned and ran. I was not going to be deterred by Drake screaming for me to come back. Almost falling down the stairs, I caught myself on the railing in time to break the fall. I was out of breath by the time I reached my dorm. Confused and heartbroken, I went into my room and threw myself across the bed. Laying in the fetal position, I tried to make sense of why Drake would hurt me so.

If he didn't want to wait on me, he should have just been honest about it! I thought. To catch him with Autumn like that caused me so much misery. I wished I hadn't gone to his room. Then, I wouldn't have that horrible picture of him screwing her in my head. I knew Autumn wanted him all along, I just didn't know her feelings were reciprocated by him. I thought his love for me was stronger than that.

The ringing of the phone startled me out of my musing. Knowing it would be Drake, I didn't answer it. He kept calling for about fifteen minutes.

I really needed Denise, but I didn't bother her on her date. Pulling myself off the bed, I pulled off my clothes and let them fall in a pile on the floor. I didn't care about anything. I was just numb. I cut on the water and made it as hot as I could stand it, hoping it would wash away my numbness.

Putting on my shower cap, I stepped under the hot spray. Grabbing my sponge, I soaped my entire body with my favorite bath gel. After finishing my shower, I stepped out and oiled my body from head to toe before I was fully dried. I glanced at myself in the mirror. I wasn't Autumn Blake, but I wasn't chopped liver either!

Although I could stand to lose 25 or 30 pounds, the mirror reflected beautiful, smooth caramel skin, full C-cup breasts and well-rounded thick hips. Pulling on my nightshirt and panties, I climbed into bed. All I wanted to do was forget I ever met Drake. I knew he was too good to be true. All guys that fine were.

Trying hard to stifle my continuous flow of tears, I heard a loud banging on the door.

"Open the door Alyssa, baby," Drake's slurred speech shouted through the door.

Grabbing a pillow to cover my ears, I ignored him. As he got louder and louder, I knew it would only be a matter of time before security came. I didn't want to cause a scene, so I let him in against my better judgment.

Opening the door, I tugged down my nightshirt that came above my knees. "Please, keep it down Drake! Do you want to get into trouble?"

"I don't care what happens to me, Alyssa, as long as you hear me out."

"Drake, I really don't need to hear anything from your mouth. I saw what I saw and that is all I can handle right now!"

"Alyssa, please hear me out. I..."

Cutting him off, I said, "I do have one question. Why did you lie and say you would wait on me when you had no intention of waiting to have sex? You promised me you didn't want her! You knew my dislike of her and how she was always flirting with you. I had my reservations about her from the jump, but you reassured me there was nothing to worry about." I was on a roll and had to breathe to control the anger that rose up in me like a volcano near eruption.

"Baby, listen to me, please. I was studying so hard tonight and I needed a break. Autumn and I were studying for Professor Grant's class. Everyone knows what a hard ass he can be. She suggested we buy some beer, and we were just going to chill for a while. I admit I drunk more than I should have on an empty stomach. One thing led to another and I am ashamed I let things go that far. I am also hurting, because I brought this hurt on us. I was weak baby, but I can promise you this is the first and only time I messed up since we've been together. You have to believe that, if you believe nothing else. I'm hoping you will find it in your heart to forgive my idiotic mistake. It will not happen again."

"I don't believe a word coming out your mouth," I said cutting Drake off again. "But, you can tell me another thing. Did you use protection?" He looked away with regret, and I already knew his answer. "How stupid could you be, Drake? And to think, I was coming over to give myself to you tonight."

He stood there with a dumbfounded look on his face. "Baby, I'm sorry," he said and attempted to touch me, but I jerked away.

"I hate you! I will never be with you. Do you understand how much you hurt me? I feel as if someone has died. You will never get the chance to hurt me again!"

He dropped to his knees with tears streaming down his handsome face, and it was almost my undoing when he grabbed me around the waist and wet my nightshirt with his tears. "Alyssa, you have to forgive me," he begged. Reaching into his pocket, he took out a little black box and opened it. Inside laid a beautiful four-carat square-cut solitaire. He attempted to place the ring on my finger.

"Baby, I was going to ask you to marry me on the day of my graduation. But, I can't wait. Alyssa Darden will you marry me?"

16

"How romantic? You ask me to marry you a few minutes after another woman just crawled off of you. I can still smell her stench on you. How dare you?" The more I screamed my anger at him, the more the tears flowed. Not caring that my nose was running, I took the back of my hand and wiped as much as I could with the sleeve of my shirt. "Get out, Drake! Get out this very minute."

Defeated, he stood up from his bended knee. "Alyssa, please don't do this to us."

"You only have two more weeks before graduation and, in that time, I don't want you to come near me! If we cross paths, don't you dare look at me. Turn and go the other way. If you do, I promise you, I won't be responsible for my actions."

"Please Alyssa, let me make this right. Give me one more chance, baby."

"How could you possibly make this right, Drake?"

"You know, I got drafted by the Dallas Cowboys," he said pulling me close to him. "They signed me to a five-year contract. You

17

could stay here and finish school, and I'll make arrangements to have you flown out to as many games you will be able to attend. I have a 16.5 million dollar five-year contract. I will take care of you and you can finish college without worrying about your finances."

Pushing him away in disgust, I turned my back to him. I took a deep breath to compose my next words. I turned and looked directly into those beautiful hazel eyes. I saw the remorse there, but I couldn't let what happen tonight slide. "Drake, you could make all the money on God's green earth, and I still would not marry you. I'm going to tell you one last time, I want you to leave. If you love me the way you say you do, leave me the hell alone! Never try to contact me again, because my answer will still be the same."

I heard keys jiggling at the door. Denise entered the room giggling about something Weston was saying. Seeing Drake and I standing in the middle of the room and me with tear streaks and a snotty nose, Denise ran to me. "What's wrong?" she asked.

I burst into tears again. "Please, make Drake leave!"

Not understanding what was going on, she followed my wishes and insisted that Weston take Drake and leave.

"Come on man. I don't know what's going on, but let's go somewhere and talk," Weston said as he pushed Drake out of the door.

Looking back at me with puppy dog eyes, Drake said, "I love you and will never give up on us."

In a fit of anger, I shouted, "You gave up on us when you screwed that bitch, Autumn!" I ran into my bedroom and slammed the door behind me.

Denise knocked and entered the room without waiting for a response. "Now, tell me what's going on? What do you mean Drake slept with Autumn?"

Pulling myself together, I explained how I decided to surprise Drake tonight at his dorm and what I walked in on.

"Oh my God! I am so sorry, Lyssa! I can't imagine what you are going through. I ought to kick both of their dirty dog butts myself. And, I can't believe the nerve of Autumn. She had to seduce him. She is a slut and everyone knows how bad she wanted him. The nerve of her!"

"I can't put this all on her, Denise. Drake was responsible for his own actions. He could have said no. Girl, and on top of that he didn't even use protection. How stupid can he be?" I asked with renewed anger in my voice.

"Alyssa, he told me before he left that he asked you to marry him. Now, I understand why you turned him down. Men can be so stupid sometimes. What? Did he expect for you to fall all over him and accept his proposal?"

"I don't think he's that delusional. He got the picture that I want nothing to do with him now or in the future."

"I hate to tell you this while you are down, but Weston proposed to me tonight, too. And I said yes!"

"That's great, Denise! You never have to apologize for being happy. I'm happy for you," I said reaching over and giving her a hug. "Is that the ring on your finger?"

"Yes," Denise said proudly displaying the princess-cut diamond on her finger.

"That is so beautiful. I am truly happy for you guys," I said as a mixture of sadness and joy swept over my spirit.

***

The next two weeks were hard. Whenever I encountered Autumn, she had a smirk on her face. I ignored her as best I could, but I still felt the sting of Drake's betrayal every time we crossed paths. I went into the Student Union building two days before Drake and Weston's graduation and saw him and Autumn sitting together at one of the tables. I really didn't need to see that right then, so I turned to leave. Drake spotted me before I could quietly exit the building.

"Alyssa wait up!" he called out. I kept walking like I didn't hear him. He caught up to me and said, "Alyssa, I know you hear me calling you. If you didn't see me why are you walking away so fast?"

With fire in my eyes, I turned and confronted him. "We have nothing to say to each other. We have said all we need to say to each other. Besides, you have the right company to occupy your time," I said as I gestured to Autumn.

"It's not what you think! We were going over some last minute graduation stuff. That is all. Will you please come over to the table with me? I want to address what happened out in the open, so we can put this whole thing behind us."

I looked at him as if he'd lost his mind. "Did you not hear anything I said in our conversation the other week? We are through, nada, no more! We have nothing to talk about. I wish you well in your life with whatever you do. Just do it without me... Goodbye Drake!" I walked away leaving him staring at my back with a hopeless look on his face.

His graduation day came, and the only reason I was in attendance was because

Weston was graduating, too. I wanted to give him my support. Denise wouldn't have forgiven me for missing her man's event. But, as soon as it was over, I congratulated Weston and left. They were very understanding about why I didn't want to go to the after party.

Entering my dorm building, I found Drake waiting for me outside of my door. "Alyssa, I know you want nothing to do with me right now, but please hear me out. I love you and I want you to be my wife. Please, I am begging you to try to find forgiveness in your heart for me. Slap me, hit me, just do what you got to do to get this anger out your system so we can get past this and move on together."

"Drake, I am not going to lie. Yes, I still love you. I really do. I just can't forget this right now. I can't be with you right now. Yes, we can move on, just not with each other."

As I opened my door to enter my dorm, he grabbed me around my waist and spun me around. Placing one palm on my face, he lowered his thick lips to mine. I closed my eyes and blocked out his serious hazel gaze. I allowed him to kiss me one last time. It was so easy to get lost in his sensuous kiss. Slipping his tongue between my lips, he twirled it with mines. I breathed in his essence, so I could remember the smell and feel of him. God only knew how much I loved that man. Sliding his hands down to my hips, he widened my stance, so I could feel his hardness pressing against me.

"Alyssa, baby please let me make love to you. Let me love you. I want... No, I need you so damn bad."

Snapping myself out of the building passion, and back to reality, I pushed Drake away from me. Pictures of him and Autumn rushed through my head. I wondered were those the same words he said to her when they were together.

"Goodbye Drake! I can't and I won't go through this with you, ever again." With that said, I let myself into my room and began my life without Drake Peterson.

Chapter 1

There I was twelve years later, standing outside Denise and Weston's house on the beautiful and scenic Magnolia Avenue. Ringing that doorbell was one of the hardest things I'd ever done. It was my first time going to Denise's beautiful home and she wouldn't be there to greet me. How ironic was that? Squaring my shoulders, I pressed the doorbell and hoped I could be strong and not fall apart.

Weston opened the door and gathered me into his arms in a warm hug. I took comfort in his arms. They made me feel closer to Denise, whom I missed then more than ever.

"Weston, I am so sorry I wasn't here for Denise. Why didn't she tell me she was sick? She had to know I wouldn't have let her go through this alone."

Inviting me in, he led me to his living room and offered me a seat on the plush sofa. He took the matching chair across from me.

"Alyssa, those were Denise's wishes. When she found out she had breast cancer a year ago, she did everything she could do to fight it. She didn't want people treating her differently. She wouldn't have wanted you to uproot your life for her. She wanted you to remember her for who she was and not the diseased shell of a body she had become."

"Weston, you know she was more than a friend to me. She was like a sister to me. I shouldn't have stayed away so long and I will feel guilty until my dying day."

Taking my hands into his, he said, "Alyssa you knew Denise about as well as I did, and you know she wouldn't want you to feel that way."

"I know. You are so right. I just need a minute to wrap my head around the fact that she is gone. How are the girls holding up? Where are they?"

"They are with their grandmother. She picked them up this morning wanting to get them out of the house for a while. It's hard on Alisha and Alexis. Hell, it's hard on me. That woman was my soul mate... the love of my life. If it wasn't for my girls, I don't know what I would do. I have to go on for them." Weston changed the subject and caught me up on a lot that had been going on since I moved away. Since I was there, I realized how much I missed calling that place home. It was so much different than the hustle and bustle of New York. "Alyssa, why aren't you married yet? I was sure you would have been married and had a kid or two by now," he said.

"I am seeing someone and have been for a while now. His name is David McRay. I really think we are good together. He hasn't popped the question yet, but I got a feeling he will soon."

"Are you ready for marriage if he asks you?"

"To be honest, I don't know. I really do care for him a lot. I just don't know if I'm ready.

27

What I do know is that I definitely want children, I'm 34 years old and my clock is ticking."

"Don't get mad at me, Lyssa," Weston said reverting back to my nickname in college.

"Go ahead, Wes," I said with a smile. "Say what's on your mind?"

"Well, I've just always wondered what it would have been like if you would have forgiven Drake. Maybe you could have been happy and we could have raised our kids together, just like the way you and Denise grew up together."

"The past is the past," I said. "Besides, Denise told me he married Autumn. I mean, she did get pregnant after he slept with her, remember? I have to hand it to her, she went after what she wanted and got it."

"He married her and divorced her," Weston said with a smirk.

"I'm sorry to hear that," I said, surprised that I really meant it. "It's sad when children are involved in a divorce. Their son should be around eleven by now right?"

"Something like that. He is about four years older than the twins."

Pointedly, I changed the subject. "When was the last time you've eaten? I am kind of famished after passing on the air plane food."

"Forgive my manners, what do you want to drink? There is plenty of food in the fridge that friends and neighbors have been bringing over."

"Thank you, but why don't we go to my favorite restaurant. I saw it on my way over here."

"No need to say more," Wes said with a smile." Applebees here we come. I didn't forget."

Chapter 2

"Hi, I'm Sarah, and I will be your waitress." Arriving at Applebees, we went in and was shown to our table by our waitress. After we were seated, she handed us menus and took our drink order. She left to go get our iced tea while we perused the menu. I decided on the spinach dip for starters and for my main dish I chose fried shrimp and baked potato with a side salad. Weston decided on the same. However, instead of shrimp, he ordered the rib eye steak. When our dinner arrived and our drinks were refilled, we dove in to satisfy our hunger.

"I really appreciate you being here, Alyssa. This is the most I've eaten since Denise died."

"I wish I had come sooner. Had I known she was ill, I would have come sooner. You know

Wes, I shouldn't have let this be the reason to bring me home. Even though Dad is gone, you and Denise were still like family. I really missed you all. I missed seeing your babies born. Don't get me wrong, I love that you sent me pictures over the years. I'm just feeling overly sentimental right now. I never realized how much I missed the place where I grew up, until now."

"I knew how hurt you were when your dad died during your last year of college. That couldn't have been easy for you. Denise and I understood you wanting to start fresh somewhere else. We knew you never got over what happened with Drake. Finding out that Autumn was pregnant by him didn't help make matters any better."

"The past is the past, so let's just leave it where it belongs. I'm enjoying my life in New York. I have a wonderful man in my life who I think loves me. I enjoy teaching and I love my kids. Who could ask for anything more?"

"That's great, Alyssa! You deserve to be happy." Finishing his meal, Weston insisted on paying the bill, even though I tried to take care of it myself.

When we arrived back at his house, I dropped him off and promised to see him the next day, which was the day of the funeral. All I wanted to do when I reached the hotel was crawl into bed and sleep until morning. I pulled off my clothes, put on my nightgown and crawled between the crisp clean sheets. I was out like a light within minutes.

The next morning, I called room service and ordered a light breakfast. I showered and put on a matching baby blue lacy bra set with matching lace panties. I slipped on a short-sleeved fitted black dress with a squared neck. Slipping my stocking-covered feet into three-inch black heels, I put on a pair of pearl drop earrings with a matching necklace. On my way out the door, I grabbed my black clutch and cell.

The funeral was very sad. I said my last goodbyes to one of the most gentle and loving people I knew. The church was packed with friends and family. At the cemetery, with friends and family holding white balloons, we released them to the heavens where I knew Denise's soul would abide with God for all of eternity.

Taking one last look at the gravesite, I turned and almost lost my balance as I came face to face with Drake Peterson. There were so many people there that I hadn't seen him in the crowd. Through teary eyes, I could see that he was standing tall and more handsome than the last time I saw him. It should have been a sin how fine he was. His wavy hair was cut close to his scalp. Those beautiful hazel eyes of his were still as I remembered. He was more handsome in his maturity than he was in college. Grabbing me by my shoulders, he pulled me into his strong and still muscular arms.

"Alyssa! I wasn't sure you would be here, but I should never have doubted that you would be. I am so glad to see you again, even if it is under such sad circumstances. I know how close you and Denise were."

For the first time that day, I smiled. Drake

smelled so good it took everything in me to remember where I was. My heart rate increased as all the love I thought was gone forever resurfaced as if it was awaking from a deep sleep. I had to get control over my emotions. I had David back in New York and he was safe and dependable. Pulling myself out of Drake's arms, I smiled hoping he didn't see in my eyes how much he had unsettled me.

"It is good to see you too, Drake," I said in a calm voice.

"Wow! You look beautiful. You are more beautiful than the last time I saw you, if that's possible."

"Thank you," I said as his eyes devoured me where I stood. I needed to get as far away from Drake as possible, because the way I responded to him was not good. "Drake it's good seeing you, but I am going to go on over to Weston's place and spend some time with the family before I go back to my hotel."

"Great! I'm going by there, so I'll definitely see you there," he said. "Where are you parked? I'll walk you to your car," he insisted.

Leading the way to my rental, I turned and saw Drake staring at my rear, which made me walked faster to the parked car. I unlocked the door with my key pad and Drake reached around me and opened the door. I slid behind the wheel and was about to thank him when I noticed his eyes were glued to my thighs where my dress had ridden dangerously high. I cleared my throat to get his attention, so he would close the door. He closed the door he stepped back. He did not try to hide the look of total lust in his eyes.

"Thanks."

"You are most definitely welcome, Alyssa."

"I guess I'll see you at Weston's," I said as he stepped back from the car.

"That you will," he said with a cute tilt to his lips before turning and heading in the direction of his vehicle.

Chapter 3

After arriving back at Weston's, I went in and greeted his family. Alexis and Alisha looked just like their mother. They were beautiful eight-year-old twins. There I was, their Godmother, and I'd only interacted with them through pictures, the many gifts I sent through the years, and phone conversations here and there. There was nothing more beautiful than to see two mini Denise's in the flesh.

"Hello," I said when they looked up at me with identical expressions of sadness. "I'm your mommy's oldest and dearest friend," I said as I took a seat between them.

"I know who you are. You send us all those

cool gifts for our birthdays and holidays," Alisha said showing off her missing front tooth.

"Yeah! We talk to you on the phone, too," Alexis piped in.

"Yes, you do," I said with a gentle smile. "Can you two do me a big favor?"

"What?" they asked in unison.

"Well, I really could use a couple of hugs right now. Do you think you two can give me one?"

I didn't have to ask twice. Both hugged me with their little arms as if their lives depended on it. It took everything in me to hold back the tears threatening to fall. As I sat there talking to the girls, the short hairs on the back of my neck stood up. Without turning around, I knew Drake had entered the room.

When they spotted him, Alisha and Alexis jumped to their feet and ran to bombard him with hugs and kisses. They each took his hands and led him over to the sofa where I was still seated. "Uncle Drake, do you know mommy's best friend?" asked Alexis.

"Yes, sweetheart, Alyssa and I go way back."

Before I could excuse myself, the girls decided to go look for their father.

"You mind if I sit here?" Drake asked pointing to the spot on the sofa beside me. Not giving me a chance to answer, he sat beside me brushing his leg against mine as he sat. His cologne assailed my nostrils and for the second time in an hour my heart was racing. It wasn't even hot in the house, yet I could feel a trickle of sweat ease down my spine. I was uncomfortable with the way my body reacted to him. "I hear you're still living in New York. Do you like it there?" he asked.

"Yes, I like it very much."

"Are you happy?" he asked looking deep into my eyes, as if he really needed to know.

"I think I'm happy. I have a couple of good friends. I make a living at something I love, and that's teaching kids. I have a boyfriend who loves me. I'm healthy... What more could I ask for?"

"Do you love your boyfriend?"

"Drake, I think you're getting a little too personal. Not that it's any of your business, but I care for David a lot."

I was so glad when Weston came over to join our conversation. We talked a while about old times and the good times we use to have. After many stories, tears, and laughs had been shared, I looked at my watch and saw that it was getting late. I also noticed most of the guests had already left.

I stood up and picked up my clutch. "Wes, I really hate to leave, but I have a ten o'clock flight tomorrow morning," I said and then hugged Wes and said my goodbyes to the twins, while Drake stood silently by. Turning lastly to him with a half attempt to smile, I said, "It was good to see you, too, Drake."

"It is getting late, so I'm about to leave too," he said returning a full smile of his own. Then, in a serious tone, he added, "But, before you go, I really want to talk to you."

I noticed Alisha and Alexis looking on in rapt interest. Even Weston was smiling from ear to ear as he waited to see how I would answer.

"I promised Wes that I wouldn't stay away so long again, so maybe another time. I really do have to pack and get ready to leave tomorrow."

"I'll tell you what. Why don't I follow you back to the hotel and we can grab a drink at the bar. One drink. Then, you can call it a night." Drake was not one to take no for an answer.

"Okay, one drink," I said thinking one drink would be okay. I would hear him out and then send him on his way.

Drake and I said our goodbyes and saw ourselves out. Once we arrived at the hotel, I told him that I had a mini bar in my room that was fully stocked. "Do you want to just have drinks there?" I asked. I was tired. The emotions of the day had finally caught up with me, so I foolishly suggested that we talk in my room instead of the dimly lit bar.

"We can talk on the street, in the bar or in the room. I just want to talk to you, Alyssa."

I opened the door, and Drake followed me into the hotel room. "The bar is over there," I said nodding in the direction that hid a mini fridge behind it. "Help yourself to what's there and I'll be back shortly."

I went into the bedroom and closed the door behind me. I reached inside my purse and pulled out my cell. I had several missed calls from David. I had forgotten to turn my cell back on and he was probably worried. Punching in his number, I wondered should I tell him about Drake. Then again, there wasn't anything to tell.

"Hey babe," he said when he answered.

"Hi David. I'm so sorry I didn't call you sooner. I know it's late there, but I wanted you to know that I'm okay."

"I wish you would have let me come with you. I feel bad you're there all alone. I'm your man and I should be there comforting you through this."

"You are so sweet, but you just received your promotion. I know how busy you've been and how hard you worked for that promotion. Plus, all those crazy hours you keep at the bank. How would you have found time to come with me?"

"You're right, baby. I just wanted to be there for you. You know how much I love you, right Alyssa?"

"Of course, I do and you know how I feel, too. Listen, I'm going to get off this phone and I'll see you when you pick me up at the airport tomorrow."

Disconnecting the call, I sat on the edge of the bed and removed my heels. While taking off my clothes and putting on pajama bottoms with a matching T-shirt, I thought about David. He was a little shorter than Drake. And, where Drake was dark, he was just the opposite. He was the color of cafe au lait with green eyes and curly hair. You could tell he was of mixed heritage just by looking at him. He was dependable and I felt blessed to have him in my life.

Upon going back out to where Drake sat patiently waiting with our drinks poured, I saw he had a glass of wine for me. For him, he had something dark in a glass with no ice. His suit jacket and tie were on the arm of the sofa. I hoped he was not getting too comfortable.

"Now that we are nice and comfortable, let's talk," I said sarcastically.

He took a healthy swallow of his drink and sat the glass down on the table in front of him. I took a seat on the other end of the sofa and reached for my glass of wine and began sipping.

"First, I wanted to say that I was so sorry I didn't make it back here when your dad died. I really wanted to be here for you. I was on the road and there was no way I would have made it in time for the funeral."

"I still miss dad a lot. I admit that sometimes I feel so alone in this world without him around. But, you had a wife and a child to take care of. Denise and Weston never left my

44

side. If it hadn't been for those two, I don't think I would have made it."

"Alyssa, don't you know that nothing would have kept me from coming to you in your time of need if I had been able to help it?"

"Not even your wife?" I emphasized the word *wife*.

"No, not even her," he said as his eyes burned into mine.

"Well, I got the flowers," I said averting my eyes to look at my nails as if they had answers as to why my heart kept fluttering every time I looked into Drake's hazel eyes. "Thank you for those. I remember that they were beautiful."

"Why aren't you married, Alyssa?"
"You sound just like Weston."

I shrugged my shoulders. "I've never been ready, I suppose. I must admit that lately I've been thinking about kids. So, when and if David asks me, I'm thinking about accepting."

Drake's eyes were unreadable as he looked at me. "We could have been married with a house full of kids if you had married me. We would have had beautiful children together."

"How soon do we forget? How would I have fit into the equation? You were having a baby with Autumn, remember?"

"Alyssa, be real! Do you truly believe I would have married her if you gave me a chance? Baby or no baby, I would have married you in a heartbeat. Don't get me wrong, I would have manned up and took care of my child. But, woman, it was you I loved. It's you that I will always love. You weren't even there in Dallas with us, but you was always in my marriage. It was you that I had in my heart!"

This man! He was resurrecting buried feelings that I wanted like hell to stay buried.

"Drake, can we please change the subject?" I begged while downing the rest of my wine in one gulp. "What's done is done. I've moved on with my life with David. I can't... I won't go back. For God's sake, what we had happened twelve years ago!"

"Baby, who are you trying to convince?" he asked as he slid over on the sofa and invaded my space; he was much too close. "Tell me truthfully, do you really love this man?"

He was so close that I could feel his breath on my lips. I could see the gold flecks in his eyes. I wanted to run my fingers over his close-cropped wavy hair so bad that I clenched my hands tight to stop myself.

"Wait... Now... Who are you to ask me those type of questions? How much I love David isn't any of your damn business, and stop calling me baby," I said snapping out of Drake Peterson's trance. I took a deep breath and folded my arms.

"Don't make me prove you wrong, Lyssa. You were my baby once and I can make you again. Don't think I haven't noticed the way you look at me. That hungry look in your eyes is the same one I have in mine."

"I do not!" I knew I was lying to myself as soon as the words came out my mouth.

A wild gleam I never saw before entered Drake's eyes. He sat back onto the sofa and his strong arms pulled me onto his lap. Raking his hands through my shoulder length hair, he pulled my face to his. Looking deeply into my eyes, he crushed his thick lips onto mine. His other hand was around my waist to hold me in place.

I snaked my arms around his neck and our lips came together like we were coming home. We kissed with a pent up longing that had been buried for twelve long years. I didn't have it in me to put up a fight. I wanted him just as bad as he wanted me. For that one night, I would not lie to myself again.

He began to explore my body with his hands. Pulling my shirt over my head, he placed his hands on my full lush breasts. When his warm hands brushed over my nipples, it sent an electric charge straight to my core.

What am I doing? I asked myself a question that went right out of my mind when I felt his big hand ease inside my pajama bottoms. Finding my ripe bulb, his bold touch made my juices flow heavy. I could feel his steel hard arousal against my backside as I squirmed on his lap.

He groaned against my soft lips. Taking his tongue, he licked my lips as if he was licking a lollipop. Burying his face against my neck, he bit and sucked in an attempt to leave his mark. By then, I was so far gone I didn't try to stop him. I relished the sharp sting of his teeth on my neck. Hopefully, I wouldn't have to explain the marks to David.

Laying me onto the sofa, Drake pulled my pajama bottoms off. He kneeled onto the soft plush carpet and slid my bottom to the edge of the sofa. Diving in, he inhaled my essence and groaned at the same time. "You smell so damn good, baby," he said as he placed a tender kiss

49

on my thigh.

I almost jumped out of my skin when I felt the first flick of his tongue against my clit. Taking two fingers, he placed them inside of my canal and I came all over his tongue and mouth. He moaned as he slurped my juices, taking every drop into his mouth. Standing, he removed his clothes with urgency.

Standing before me in only snug black briefs, my eyes widened. Judging from his imprint, he was huge! *What have I gotten myself into?* I thought. And, as if he read my reaction, he pulled me into his embrace and assaulted my lips once again with raw passion.

Running my hands down his muscular shoulders made me want that man with an intensity I couldn't control. At that moment, I didn't want to control it. I had to feel him! Reaching inside his briefs, I took hold of the very thing I craved to feel deep inside of me. I moaned as I anticipated the pleasure he would bestow upon me. With a guttural moan, he removed my hand, pushed down his briefs and stepped out of them.

"I can't wait Alyssa! I have to have you now."

I took in his magnificent body. Flat washboard abs and strong toned thighs. Then, I looked at my thick thighs and soft belly and became unsure of my image. Once again, as if knowing my thoughts, he took my chin into his hands and looked directly into my eyes and said, "Baby, you are so beautiful. You are perfection in my eyes from your pretty little head to the soles of your feet."

Blushing, I tried to turn my head away, but he wouldn't let me. Putting a hand between my legs, he continued to look into my eyes. "I've only had one taste of you and I am already addicted. I love you, Alyssa! I never stopped, and I know you have feelings for me. Please, tell me if I'm wrong."

"Drake, I can't talk about this right now," I said as my eyes glazed over with passion while his fingers continued to move inside of me.

He laid me down and kissed me with a ferocity that had me whimpering and pleading for him to enter me. "Whether you admit it or not, you tell me with your looks and the way you are responding to me right now."

"Make love to me, Drake."

Opening my legs, he answered my request and entered me with great restraint, because of his large size. "Oh baby... You're so tight. Don't move! I don't want this to be over before I start." Draping one leg onto his shoulder, he entered me deeper. As I stretched to accommodate his size, he began taking long, slow strokes that I met stroke for stroke.

When he took my nipple into his mouth, I could feel my orgasm build as our slick bodies slapped together in raw need. I gave into a strong orgasm that toppled over into mini contractions that caused Drake to let out a loud groan as he spilled his hot seed inside of me. I remembered in that moment that we hadn't used any protection. I tried to push him off me, but he wouldn't budge. Instead, he began to kiss me and I felt him hardening once again. I relaxed and gave in to Drake Peterson once again without allowing thoughts of the repercussions tomorrow would bring.

After he made love to me one final time, I passed out from sheer pleasure. The next morning, I woke up in bed with Drake's arms wrapped tightly around my waist. I glanced at the clock on the wall. It was 9:35 A.M. I had to get up and get moving if I wanted to catch my flight and return the rental car to the airport.

Easing from Drake's arms, I tried not to wake him. I wanted to be showered and fully dressed before I had to face him again. Being quiet as possible, I grabbed my toiletries and clothes and headed for the shower. Once fully dressed, and with my teeth brushed, I entered the room to find Drake awake and looking delicious as he lay there wrapped in the hotel's white sheets. I wanted to crawl back into the bed and make love to him all over again. But, common sense prevailed. I knew in my heart that it could never happen again.

"Good morning beautiful. I could get used to waking up to you every morning."

"Good morning," I replied, ignoring the last part of his statement. I was also trying not to look at his morning erection, which could be seen through the sheet.

"Come back to bed, Alyssa."

"No. I have to get going," I said and then looked away. "And... Thank you for last night, but this can never happen again. Let's just chalk this mistake up to us finally having closure."

Getting out of the bed in all of his naked glory, he turned me to face him and enclosed my hands in his. "I know you aren't trying to dismiss last night as a mistake. Stop lying to yourself. You know that the two of us being together never was and will never be a mistake. This was fate. Fate brought us back together. It took sad circumstances to bring us to this point, but it brought us together nonetheless."

"Well, we were together and now I am leaving," I said as I began to pack my things.

"Please, don't hold on to how I hurt you in the past. I was hoping the passing years would allow you the time to forgive me one day."

"No Drake, I'm not holding on to the past. I am just living in the moment we are in where I have a boyfriend and you have a wife. Now, could you please put some clothes on?"

"Ex-wife," Drake said as he walked to the bathroom.

While he showered and dressed, I used that

time to finish packing. I waited for him on the sofa where we started our lovemaking the night before. When he came out of the bedroom, thankfully he was fully dressed. I knew leaving him wouldn't be easy, but I had no other options. My life was in New York. David, a man I was supposed to love and be faithful to, was there waiting for me. Breathing deeply, I laid my cards on the table for Drake.

"I'm just going to get straight to the point. I was so wrong on so many levels for sleeping with you. I would never want to hurt David, for one. I remember what that kind of hurt feels like."

"Alyssa, are you telling me that you can just go back home and forget what happened between us? I don't think it will be that easy, sweetheart. I will do anything to make you mine again. I am older and so much wiser, and I promise you that I won't do anything to mess up what we have again. Just give us another chance."

"I can't just start up with you, just like that," I said snapping my fingers. "Please, accept my decision. Besides, I have to go or I will be late making it to the airport. If I want to make my flight on time, I really need to leave now." I slung my shoulder bag onto my shoulder and attempted to grab the handle to pull my luggage, but Drake took them both from me.

"I got it. Let's go," he said with hurt in his eyes.

Taking the elevator down to the lobby, I returned the key to the front desk and we were out the door. The sun was blazing. The day was gorgeous, yet I had a heavy heart that was so torn. I popped the trunk, so he could store my luggage. I stood on the driver's side trying to hold in tears that were threatening to fall.

"Here take my card," he said handing it to

me. "All of my contact numbers are on there. You can call me for anything; it doesn't matter what time of day or night." Taking his card, I slid it into my purse. "Now, can I have your number? I need to stay in touch, if only to see how life is treating you," he said.

Since he put it that way, I didn't see any harm in him having my cell. "It's 555-737-5065," I said as he entered it into his phone.

"This is not goodbye," he said and pulled me into his arms. His eyes were glassy as he embraced me like he never wanted to let me go. "I will never say goodbye to you again baby," he whispered against my ear.

"I really need to leave, Drake." My emotions were getting the best of me. I knew, if I broke down in front of him, there would be no way in hell he would let me leave. Before letting me go, he made me promise to let him know when I arrived. I agreed to call him when I got home and slid behind the wheel.

He shut the door and stared at me through the window with his hands deep in his pockets. He almost looked lost.

Waving one last time, I backed out. I looked in my rear view mirror, and Drake stood in the same spot as he watched me disappear from sight.

Chapter 4

Finally letting my tears fall, I took I-85 North and headed toward the airport that would carry me far away from Drake, and back to David who I hoped would never find out about what I had done. I never wanted to cause the same kind of hurt and betrayal to another person. I experienced that hurt at one time in my life and I was no better than Drake who did it to me all those years ago. What I did was even worse, because I was a full-grown woman who shouldn't have given in to her lusts. All those thoughts went through my head as I landed at the JFK and into the arms of the man waiting for me. Once I'd claimed my baggage, I turned and David was right there waiting in a Charcoal gray suit cut to perfection. He always dressed like the professional that he was.

"I am so glad to see you," he said.

Rushing into his arms, I dropped my luggage and wrapped my arms around his neck as he spun me around. He looked into my eyes and settled his trimmed mustached mouth onto mines. Returning his kiss, I realized that I was really happy to see him. "Thank you so much for picking me up. I know how busy things can get at the bank, Mr. Vice President," I said with a smile.

He had gotten promoted about six months before at Liberty National Bank of NYC. I was very proud of his achievements.

Placing me on my feet, he picked up my bags and we walked out of the airport to his

Black SUV parked at the curb. Soon, we arrived at my Park Slope Apartment, which was located in the Western section of Brooklyn. I lived in a nice neighborhood, although my apartment was quite small. It consisted of a kitchen, setting room, bedroom and bathroom. I couldn't afford a bigger place on my teacher's pay, but I was happy to have a place of my own.

"David, you can put my bags in the bedroom. I'll unpack later," I told him.

I was glad that it was Friday. That gave me the whole weekend to recoup and get ready for my second grade class on Monday morning. David returned and sat on the sofa where I was sitting. He pulled my feet into his lap and slid off my shoes so he could massage my feet.

"I'm sorry I didn't take time off to travel with you to your friend's funeral. I know it had to be hard on you, baby."

"What was hard was watching Weston and the girls look so lost and sad. It broke my heart knowing that Alexis and Alisha will grow up without their mother. I was only a little older than them when I lost my mother. I still miss her to this day."

"Baby, I know you have to be worn out. Why don't you go and soak in the tub and I'll run to your favorite Chinese restaurant and get you some sesame chicken with rice."

"You are so sweet to me. Thank you!"

Pulling my feet from his lap, he stood and pulled me into his arms. He kissed my lips with such tenderness. "I'll be back as quick as I can. Lock up behind me and I'll let myself in if you're still in the tub when I get back."

After David left, I filled the bathtub with warm water and poured in a generous amount of bubble bath. As I was stripping off my clothes, my cell started to ring. Hurrying back into the bedroom, I answered before it went to voicemail.

"Alyssa, this is Drake. I just wanted to check on you to make sure you landed safely."

"Yes, I'm home now. I'm sorry I didn't call like I promised. I'm just so tired and I was about to soak in the tub for a while. May I call you back later? I really want to get my bath before the water turns cold."

"Sure, just make sure you call me back. I miss you already. I'll talk to you later," he said and disconnected the call before I could reply. I slid into the bubble-filled tub, laid my head on my bath pillow and closed my eyes. I must have dozed off, because David entered the bathroom calling my name softly.

"You look so delicious laying in all those bubbles. Do you want me to join you?" he teased.

"No." I laughed. "The water is getting cool though. Let me finish up and I'll be out in a few. Okay?"

"There are plenty of ways we can warm the water back up sweetheart, if you get my drift."

"I know, but I am starving. I will be out shortly. Now go!" I said playfully throwing water into his face.

After sliding into a pair of denim cutoffs and a graphic tee, I entered the kitchen where David had the food on plates. Sitting at the table, I quickly said grace and dug right in. I was ravenous. "David, aren't you going to sit and eat with me?"

"No baby, I wanted to get you settled. I have some paperwork that I need to finish up before I can call it a day. I'll let you rest up some tonight. Let's catch an early movie tomorrow, if you're up to it."

"That sounds great. What time should I expect you?"

"Will around six be okay? We'll grab dinner first, then go to the movies."

"That's fine David, I'll be ready."

"Come and walk your man to the door."

At the door, he encircled me in his arms. I

looked up into his green eyes as he pressed his lips to mine. Sliding his tongue between my lips, I let him pull my tongue into his mouth. As the kiss intensified, all I could remember were the kisses that Drake and I shared. All I could see were Drake's hazel eyes staring into mine. Shocked by my thoughts, I abruptly ended the kiss.

"What's wrong baby?" he asked.

"I guess I'm just overly tired. I'll see you tomorrow," I said telling the partial truth as I opened the door and pushed him out. After closing the door behind him, I leaned against it and took a deep breath.

What was I going to do? I cared for both men, in totally different ways. Drake was a love of my past that I never got over, whereas David was my "right-now" love and, given time, maybe my forever love. I never thought I would or could be in love with two men. I would always look at others who said they were and thought it was impossible. *Until the shoe is on the other foot, it's best not to judge,* I thought looking at the clock. It was a little after 8:00 PM. I walked into my bedroom and punched Drake's number on my cell. I had to end all contact with him after that call. I had to be strong and end it before someone was hurt.

Drake answered right away, as if anticipating my call. "Hey baby! I'm glad you kept your word and called me back. I would really like to see you again. I'll come to you if I have too."

"Drake, I really don't think that will be a good idea. I've had time to come to my senses. What we did was wrong and selfish of me. I am in love with David and I can't or won't hurt him no more than I already have. If he ever finds out what we did, it could be devastating."

"Alyssa, how can you say you love this David character? The passion we feel for each other couldn't be duplicated with anyone else."

"Stop it, Drake! Was the sex out of this world? Yes, it was amazing. But, a relationship can't be based on just how great the sex is alone. There has to be more there."

"Lyssa, are you telling me you don't feel any love for me? If you can tell me that you don't feel one ounce of love for me, I will leave you alone forever."

"Please, understand that I'm trying to do the best thing for all of us."

"Answer my question, Alyssa," Drake said in a demanding voice.

"I...I... just please don't call me again, Drake. If you love me, then prove it. Otherwise, let me get on with my life, a life with David. You have been divorced for several years now. Why do you want to pursue me now?"

"In all honesty baby, Weston and Denise told me how happy you were with your life there. I didn't want to come into your life and turn it upside down. You don't know how hard it was for me not to come there and claim what I know that God made just for me. The ink wasn't even dry on my divorce papers, yet all I could think about was being with you again. Hell, to be honest I would have been with you even if I wouldn't have been divorced. I restrained myself, because Denise made me promise not to hurt you again. She wanted me to leave you alone, so I did. But, when I saw you at her funeral all the bets were off. I knew I couldn't stay away from you any longer. Alyssa, if you never trust anything I say, you can trust this 100%. I have never loved any other woman but you!"

"This is all too much, Drake."

"I'm going to give you some time to think about what I said. Just know, I will not give up on us until you can convince me there is no love in your heart for me."

With tears streaming down my cheeks, all I could do was nod, even though he couldn't see me. After a few moments of silence, he said, "Good night, baby. I love you and I look forward to the day that you will be in my arms again."

Hanging up the phone, I crawled into my bed and hugged my pillow for comfort. Saturday morning, I was up bright and early. I jumped into doing my washing and weekend cleaning. After cleaning the apartment from end to end, I began to clean my fridge. I really needed a few groceries, so I pulled on my favorite old faded jeans and pulled a shirt over my head. I ran the comb through my relaxed hair before putting on socks and sneakers. Grabbing my purse, I headed out the door and walked to the corner grocery market that wasn't too far from my apartment. I lived in a neighborhood where everything was convenient and that made it plausible for me to walk to some of the places I liked to go. I could even walk, when the weather permitted, to the Park Slope Elementary School where I worked. When the weather was bad, I would take the short ride on the public transit.

Entering Henry's Grocery Market, I grabbed a cart and added eggs, milk and several other items I needed to get through the week. Mr. Henry's Grocery had been a part of that neighborhood for over twenty years. He was about 65 and had been married to his wife Marie for 40 years. They treated anyone who came through their door like family. That was why so many people liked to do their shopping there.

"Alyssa, I see you made it safely from Alabama," Mr. Henry said as I approached the counter to pay for my purchases.

"Yes, I did, Mr. Henry, and I'm glad to be home. How is Mrs. Henry Doing?"

"She was a little under the weather today. I told her to stay home and take it easy. She will be as right as rain in no time," Mr. Henry replied.

"Be sure to tell her I asked about her," I said on my way out the door with my purchases in hand.

"I will be sure to do that."

Entering my apartment, I walked to the fridge and put away my groceries. I washed my hands and got a bowl from the cabinet. I filled the bowl with Honey Nut Cheerios, grabbed a banana from my fruit bowl on the table and carried it to the living room. Sitting back on the sofa, I picked up the remote, turned to my favorite Saturday morning cartoon and immersed myself in the show while I ate. Tiring of watching television after a while, I decided to check in on Weston and the girls.

Talking with Weston and hearing the pain in his voice made me feel the loss of Denise afresh. I asked about the twins. I knew they would bring a smile to his handsome face. We talked a while about Alisha and Alexis before Weston broached the subject of Drake. "Is there anything going on between you and Drake, Alyssa?"

"No! Why would you ask that?"

"Anyone with half a brain could see there was plenty of chemistry still going on between you and Drake."

I really didn't feel comfortable lying to Wes, but I couldn't bring myself to tell him the truth either. So, unless he found out the truth from Drake, he wouldn't be hearing it from me. "We just went back to my room and talked," I said.

"Alyssa, you know I have always wanted you and Drake back together. It would be nice to have you closer, if you and Drake did decide to try again. I know it's not my business, but I just wanted you to know how I feel and, besides that, the girls just absolutely adore you."

"I love them too, Wes. Tell them I promise

to visit soon. My summer break is coming up soon and maybe I'll visit then."

"That would be great. I won't mention it to them until you make definite plans to come."

"Okay. Tell the girls hello and give them a big kiss and hug for Auntie Alyssa," I said before hanging up the phone.

After ending the call with Weston, I decided to wash my hair and give myself a mani and pedi for my date later that night. The rest of the day flew by, until David called and reminded me he would be picking me up in an hour.

After a bath, I put on black skinny jeans and paired it with a red halter top that tied at the neck. Leaving my hair to brush my shoulders in soft loose curls, I put on hoop earrings with a matching bracelet that compliment my outfit. Spraying on my favorite fragrance, *Happy* by Clinique, I stepped into black open-toe three-inch heels. The first thing

David did when he arrived was to pull me into his arms and kiss me passionately.

"We could stay here and order in if you like," he suggested.

"Well, I did want to see a movie," I said as I picked up my purse from the coffee table. I was trying to prolong being intimate with him as long as possible.

"Anything for my baby," he said opening the door. He locked up on our way out. I had to admit David looked great in his black and gold Rocawear outfit. It was a far cry from his suit and tie attire during the week. His thin mustache was shaped to perfection. His green eyes were sexy and alluring.

And, I would have been happy looking into those green eyes, if only I could stop thinking about the hazel eyes that I dreamed about every time I closed my eyes at night. I had relived our illicit encounter in my dreams. I couldn't ever let David know how another man was affecting my thoughts or let Drake know how much he had become a part of my thoughts. I needed to make things right! Starting that night, I would focus my all on David; he deserved no less.

We arrived at Rotellis and had a delicious meal that left us satisfied, but not stuffed. Their light cuisine was made to be satisfying and filling at the same time. After leaving Rotellis, we left our parked car and walked one block to the movie theater. As I laid my head on his shoulder in the darkened theater, I tried to concentrate on the movie. His hands had other ideas. I grabbed his hand to stop it from inching further up my thigh.

"David, stop it. There are too many people around."

"Okay, I'll behave." He brought our clasped hands to his lips and kissed my hand. "Do you want any popcorn or something to drink, sweetheart?"

"No," I answered as we sat back and enjoyed the movie.

After the movie, we walked back to where his SUV was parked. As he opened the door for me to get in, we heard someone calling his name. I turned toward the voice and it was a stunning, petite woman with long wavy auburn hair that stopped midway down her back. "David McRay, I thought that was you! It's been too long since I last saw you," she said coming over to him and throwing herself into his arms. Cupping David's face, all the while ignoring me standing there in plain sight, the woman had the nerve to kiss David right on the lips, leaving her ugly lipstick behind. I cleared my throat to get their attention, and he pulled her hands from his face quick and in a hurry.

"Ahh... Alyssa," he said pulling me to his side. This is Rachael Simmons. Rachael this is my girlfriend, Alyssa Darden."

Extending her fire engine red painted nails, she gave my hand a limp handshake, along with a smirky smile. All the while, she kept her gray-eyed stare on David as if she wanted to eat him alive.

"David, I just *had* to say hello when I spotted you. Now, I have to get back. I'm meeting friends and I'm sure they are waiting for me," she said as she pointed across the street at a group of ladies that I assumed were her friends.

I sneaked a peek at David to see if he was checking Rachael out like she seemed to be doing him. If he was, he wasn't obvious. I still didn't like the big goofy looking smile on his face. Rachael was handing David her business card when I returned my attention to her.

"Call me sometimes and we'll do lunch or something." She seemed to let her *or something* linger as if to imply that something could be anything he wanted. That said, she twisted her skinny tail across the street, looked back and gave David a cute little wave.

"Who the hell was that?" I asked getting into the vehicle.

Before answering, he closed my door and came around and slid behind the steering wheel.

"Rachael used to work with me at the bank. I hadn't seen her in over a year since she left the bank." Looking into my eyes before he started the car, he said, "Don't tell me you're jealous."

"Who me?" I asked with a widening of my eyes, as in how dare you think such a thing! "I am not jealous of little Miss Prissy! Do I have a reason to be?" I questioned him.

"Of course not, baby. Like I said before, we're just ex co-workers."

"Okay, then that's what it is," I replied. Thinking to myself on the drive home, I really did feel some kind of way. However, was it jealousy?

When David stopped at the traffic light, he looked at me and said, "Slide over here and give me a kiss."

"Are you serious? You still have Rachael's lipstick on your lips. It's definitely not mines, because I wear the smear proof kind."

Instead of giving him a kiss, I turned my attention to the radio and found my favorite station on satellite radio. I really didn't want to talk anymore. I did not care whether he thought I was angry or not. Going into the apartment, all I wanted to do was get ready for bed and go to sleep. David came up behind me as I laid down my purse.

"I'm ready for that kiss now," he said as he turned me towards him and lowered his lips onto mines. He'd wiped his lips clean of

Rachel's cheap lipstick.

David was a great kisser. I had to give him props on that. I also admitted that he was beginning to turn me on. Although I still felt guilty about being with Drake, I couldn't deny the attraction I felt for David.

"Let's take this to the bedroom," he whispered near my ear. Once in the bedroom, David untied my halter top and my breasts spilled into his waiting hands. Taking them to his lips, he gave each a tender kiss that had my nipples hardening and begging to be taken into his mouth.

Unzipping my jeans, he pulled my bikini panties down and off with my jeans as I stepped out of them. I sat on the bed and watched as he undressed, admiring his muscular body in the same way he was admiring me. Pushing me down onto the bed, he kissed me on the top of my head and didn't stop until he trailed warm moist kisses to the bottom of my feet. Kissing his way back to the inside of my thighs, he opened me up and deep kissed my wet heat. My hips writhed with each flick and swipe of his rough tongue. He didn't stop until my orgasm flowed into his mouth. Kissing his way further up my body, he took in my already sensitive breasts and tongued my hard nipples. Reaching into the nightstand drawer by the bed, David retrieved a condom and rolled it with haste onto his hard erection.

I knew I was wrong, but I couldn't help comparing his size and shape to Drake's. David was big, just not as big as Drake. Why couldn't I get Drake out of my head? There I was making love with my boyfriend with images of Drake creeping into my thoughts. "What's wrong baby? I feel as if you're pulling away from me," Drake said.

"I'm with you all the way, baby," I said as I pulled his lips back to mine. I really needed to focus on David, so I put more emotion into the kiss and pushed Drake into the farthest recess of my mind where he belonged and hopefully he would stay. Rolling David onto his back, I straddled him and looked into his gorgeous green eyes as I impaled myself onto his hardness. I rode him as if I was trying to finish a race.

Rolling me back under him, he slowed down the pace as if he wanted to prolong our lovemaking. Closing my eyes, I rotated my hips to meet him thrust for thrust. In total ecstasy, I bit down on my lip and succumbed to another orgasm. I had to bite my lip to keep from calling out Drake's name in the heat of the moment as yet another orgasm spiraled through me. David cried out upon his release and I was quickly brought back to my senses. Before he went into the bathroom to dispense of the condom, he kissed me once more on the lips. I was almost asleep when he crawled back into the bed and covered us.

"Goodnight David," I said as I turned my back and he pulled me to him spoon fashion. In that moment, if I was to be truthful with myself, I wished those arms around me belonged to Drake instead of David. The one man that I knew without any doubt would have the biggest portion of my heart always.

Monday morning came too soon. There were only two more weeks before school would be out for the summer. I was glad that I remembered to set my timer on the coffeemaker the night before. I needed the jolt of my morning coffee to get my day started. As always, my second graders were a handful, especially since it was so close to their summer break. It was nearly impossible to hold their attention for long. During my lunch break, I met up with a fellow teacher and good friend in the teacher's lounge.

Bernadette Terry was one of those people who said whatever was on her mind. She was a great friend to talk to, if you wanted someone who didn't bite their tongue and to tell it like it is. Straight talk no chaser. While I sat at the table eating a slice of pizza that I had gotten from the school cafeteria, Bernadette took one look at me and asked, "What's wrong, Alyssa? You look worried about something."

"Girl, I guess I'm just still tired from the trip. Don't worry about me, I'll be alright."

"This is Bernadette you're talking to, remember? Spill it girl!"

I looked at her slyly, because I knew she knew me so well. "Well... when I was in Auburn, I did something I'm not too proud of."

"Tell me and don't leave anything out," she said inching her seat closer, so we wouldn't be overheard.

"You remember years ago when we first met and I didn't want to date anyone you tried to introduce me too. Then, I told you how devastated I was when I caught my boyfriend cheating on me in college."

"Yeah, I remember all that. His name was Drake Peterson, right? The one that was the defensive lineman for the Dallas Cowboys."

"Yes, that's him, but he's retired now."

"Yeah, what about him?"

"I ran into him after Denise's funeral at the cemetery."

"What was so bad about that, Alyssa? You were bound to see people you know."

"Put a cap on it girl, and let me finish. You see after we left the cemetery, everyone went back to Weston's house for awhile. When I left Weston's house, I wasn't alone. Drake wanted to talk to me and suggested we get a drink. Instead of going somewhere public, I suggested that we have a drink in my hotel room, because I was tired. I assumed we would have one drink, air out our past and he would leave. To make a long story short, one thing led to another, and I cheated on David." I put down the half eaten pizza. I was unable to finish it.

"Girl! Men do that shit all the time, so don't beat yourself up about it. Don't let those tears fall," she said looking into my glistening eyes. "At least it was with someone you knew and not any old stranger off the street."

Shaking my head, I couldn't believe the words that came out of Bernadette's mouth. Then again, that was just like her to say something like that.

"Damn, girl! You really did it with a pro football player?"

"Ex-football player," I said starting to feel a little queasy from the pizza.

"Ex or not, I'll take him if you don't want him. That man is fine as hell. For real though, if you weren't my friend I would seriously get with him myself if I had the chance."

I couldn't help but laugh. "You are a straight up fool, you know that? If I didn't know how smart you really are Bernadette, I would seriously think about having you committed. But listen, Drake also said that he wants to see me again. It's like he just wants me to jump into a relationship with him, just like that," I said snapping my fingers for emphasis.

"What did you say about seeing him again?"

"I told him I had a very nice life here with a very nice boyfriend and I didn't want to mess that up. Drake thinks I still have strong feelings for him, too."

"Well, do you?" Bernadette asked with a serious expression.

"To be honest, yes, I still love him. I never stopped in the whole twelve years since we parted. Even when he married that skank,

Autumn, and she had his son, I still wondered what if I had forgiven him. Things could have been so different. I would have learned to love his child, given time. Hindsight is always twenty-twenty."

"Where does that leave David?"

"When I met David, as you know, I was afraid to love again. David knocked down the barriers one by one, until I fell in love with him. Bernadette, I love David. I'm just so torn."

"Don't take what I am about to say the wrong way. But, do you truly love David? It seems as if you're trying to convince yourself of your love for him, because you are scared to death of the love you have for Drake."

"I'm not trying to convince anyone of anything," I said, although there was a ring of truth in her words. Gathering my trash, I ended the conversation as lunch was almost over.

"Don't be upset, Alyssa, it was just an observation. You know your heart better than anyone."

"I know you were just trying to help. Everything is cool. I'll talk to you later," I said as I left and went to finish the remainder of my workday.

Tuesday morning, I awoke from a sleepless night of tossing and turning. I had to find the strength to prepare for the coming day. Lifting my legs out of bed and onto the floor, I sat there for a moment before pushing myself into action. Taking a quick shower before dressing, I prepared my usual bowl of cereal and banana before heading out the door to begin my work day.

Chapter 5

Back in Auburn, Drake was just opening the doors of his Boys and Girls Community Center. He was proud to be able to give back to the community after ending his football career. That was only one of several centers he had opened with his generosity. He invested his money wisely over the years. He didn't have to work another day in his life if he didn't want to. But, that was not in his nature. He was a dream maker. His dream came true the day he was drafted to play for his favorite team, the Dallas Cowboys. Therefore, he tried to open as many doors as possible for the boys and girls that entered the center doors. Entering the A & D Community Center, Drake looked around with joy in his heart. The building was a topnotch facility. It consisted of its own gym, swimming area and other rooms used for recreation, as well as tutoring. There were swimming instructors and tutors provided for the kids who needed them.

The kids wouldn't be coming until after school was let out, but he had lots of paper work on his desk that he needed to wade through. When school let out for summer break, then the center would begin its summer program. The doors would be open from 8 A.M. 'til 7 P.M.

Going to his desk and sitting in his plush leather chair, he began to think about Alyssa. He knew she needed time to come to the realization that she needed him in her life as much as he needed her. When he wanted something as bad as he wanted Alyssa, patience didn't figure into the equation. It took everything in his power not to hop a plane or pick up the phone to call her, just to hear the sound of her voice. Thinking about the sound of his name on her lips, as she called his name when they made love, had him pulling his pant leg down to make room for his girth. The ringing of the phone brought him out of his illicit thoughts.

"Hey, what's up man?" he said, identifying the caller from the caller I.D. "Weston, I'm glad that you called. I wanted to ask you had you heard anything from Alyssa since she's been home."

"Yeah, I heard from her and she is doing good. Now, I have a question for you. What's going on between you two? And, don't say nothing, because I saw the look in your eyes when you two left together. You had the look of a predator who had his eyes on the prey," Weston said with a laugh.

"Wes... Man, when I saw Alyssa the other day, it was like bam! It felt like a freight train had plowed me down where I stood. I became a man on a mission. I had to have her, at all cost. In that moment, I didn't care if she was married or had a house full of kids. I had to make her mine. I couldn't or can't lose her a second time."

"Drake, you do know she's seriously involved in a relationship right?"

"Yeah, she told me about this David guy. I didn't see a ring on her finger, so in my book she's still fair game."

"She told me she will marry this guy if and when he asks her, so that sounds like a committed relationship to me. I don't want to see Lyssa hurt again, so if you're not going to do right by her, leave her alone."

"She won't be marrying this guy, if I have anything to do with it," Drake said with authority in his voice. "The only man Alyssa will be marrying will be me, and you can mark my words on that."

"Drake, are you serious? You just can't turn her life upside down like that. She is like a sister to me, and her happiness means a lot to me. If she wants to be with you, that would be great. Just don't push her. Okay?"

"I won't do anything to hurt her. You got my word on that. I just got to come up with a plan to get her here and back into my life. This is where she belongs here with me. You need to understand just how much I love her and I never stopped. My love for her is stronger today than it ever was. Wes, if you can just understand that, man you will never question my motives again."

"You know I'm a sucker for love. I do remember how much you two loved each other until you ruined it. I will support you and her with whatever you decide, but if you hurt her again, you my boy and all, but I will personally kick your ass."

"I know you will. I was young, stupid, and thinking with the wrong head. I will never hurt her in that way, ever again. You have my word. I have a whole lot of making up to do.

Hey, give me her address, and I can start with that for starters."

Weston readily complied giving Drake the address.

"Thanks man, I owe you one," Drake said before hanging up his office phone. Picking up the phone directory with a gleam in his eyes, he put his plan into action immediately.

Chapter 6

Arriving home after a tiring day, all I wanted was a good soaking in the bathtub. The first thing I did was check the mail that had been slid through the mail slot. It was strange that I hadn't heard from David since he left early Sunday morning. It wasn't like him to go more than two days without touching base. I knew how busy he got at the bank. He said it could get mad crazy sometimes, so I decided to give him a call after my bath. As I was drying off, there was a knock at the door. I reached for my bathrobe that I kept on a hook in the bathroom, hurriedly put it on and rushed to the door. I peeped through the peephole and saw a deliveryman with a 1-800-Flowers logo on his cap. Opening the door, I came face to face with three dozen red roses.

"Good evening! Are you Miss Alyssa Darden?" the chipper deliveryman asked.

"Yes, that me." I smiled thinking of how sweet David was for sending me all those beautiful roses.

"These are for you. Where do you want me to place them?"

Leading him into my living room, I indicated he should set them on the table. "Right here, thanks. If you would wait a moment, I will give you a tip."

"No, that won't be necessary," he said as he walked to the door. "The tip has been generously taken care of. Whoever sent you these spent a pretty penny."

Smiling, I shut the door behind him. I couldn't wait to call David and thank him for the roses. I sat on the sofa and admired them as I inhaled their sweet scent. Noticing an envelope on the table that I didn't see the deliveryman leave, I picked up the letter and opened it. The card, in itself, was beautiful. Upon opening it, I saw a bold scrawl that wasn't David's handwriting but the writing of a man I was trying so hard to forget.

I see the man I can be with you right by my side. I know without a shadow of a doubt you are the only woman for me. Alyssa, please enjoy the roses, and know that I am thinking of you. All my love and all that I am, Drake.

Gasping with surprise, the card drifted from my hand and fell onto the floor. Picking up the card again, I read it once again. I was touched to my very soul with Drake's words. I picked up my cell and dialed his number that I couldn't bring myself to erase from my contact list. The call went straight to his voicemail, so I decided to leave him a brief message thanking him for the roses and to let him know how much the card meant to me. Ending the call, I went to my bedroom and pulled boy shorts with a matching tank from my dresser drawer and put them on. Fixing me a light dinner of chicken salad from the Rotisseries chicken that was already in the fridge, I added a salad and my meal was complete. I grabbed a bottle of water and sat in front of the television to watch NCIS reruns while I ate my solitary meal. As I washed my dinner dishes, my cell rang. I dried my hands on the dishtowel and answered before the call went to voicemail.

"Hello," I said seeing that it was Drake's number that appeared.

"Hey sweetheart, I'm so sorry that I missed your call. I was in a meeting that lasted a lot longer than I expected."

"I just wanted to thank you for my roses. They are so beautiful," I said as I glanced at them for the hundredth time.

"You are welcome, baby. I want to give you more and I would, if I thought you would accept more than roses."

"The roses are plenty, Drake. Please, don't start buying me things. I would feel uncomfortable taking gifts from you."

"Why would you feel uncomfortable taking gifts from me? They would be given freely. I don't expect anything in return. You already got the most important part of me and that's my heart."

"Drake please, don't say that. I don't know how you want me to respond to that."

"You respond with your heart, baby. All I want is your heart. It belonged to me once and it can again. Don't be afraid, Alyssa."

He was saying all the right things. But, I couldn't be selfish and just think of myself. I didn't want to hurt David. If David wasn't in the picture, I would have easily given Drake the answer he wanted to hear. I was having a hard enough time as it was, fighting those uncontrollable feelings for him. How long could I fight those feelings? How long did I want too? All those thoughts were going through my mind as Drake continued the one-sided conversation.

"Baby, talk to me. Don't clam up on me now," he said.

"What do you want me to say? The only thing I can offer you right now is friendship."

"I must admit, that is not the answer I wanted to hear." He was silent for a few seconds. "But, if that's all you're offering, I'll take it. You do know that friends stay in touch, right? They even get together on occasion and go out," he added.

"Okay, I can see where you are headed with this. I give you an inch and you take a yard."

Chuckling into the phone, he said, "You're damn straight."

Walking down my short hallway, I went into my bedroom and stretched into a comfortable position on the bed. I had forgotten all about calling David that night and didn't miss him not calling me. I fell asleep to the sound of Drake's deep and sexy voice. The phone somehow slid away from my grasp and was laying on the thick carpet when I awoke the next morning. Feeling refreshed from a great night's sleep, I picked the phone up from the floor and smiled as I remembered my conversation with Drake.

After a fortifying shower, I brushed my teeth and dressed in my favorite fuchsia shirt with a belted waist. I paired it with pleated black slacks. I brushed my hair out of its wrap and it brushed my shoulders. Spraying on my favorite fragrance *Happy* by Clinique, I was putting on my earrings when there was a knock at the door. *Who in the world could this be?* I thought as I opened the door. There stood David on the other side holding two cups of steaming coffee from Starbucks and a bag containing two cheese Danish.

"Hey Alyssa, I wanted to catch before you

went to work. I am so sorry that I haven't called, sweetie. You know how crazy work can get. I've been working these long crazy hours and by the time I get home at night I don't want to call and wake you." Kissing me lightly on the lips, he handed me my coffee on the way into the kitchen. Looking at the roses as he passed the living room table, next his eyes collided with mine.

Oh shit! How in the hell am I going to explain those flowers? I thought as my heart rate accelerated anticipating him asking the question I dreaded.

"Where did these come from?"

I was so glad I had removed the card or all hell would have broke loose for sure. Licking my lips that had suddenly gone dry, I said, "Ahh, an old college friend I ran into when I was in Alabama sent them."

"I wonder what kind of friend would give a

person that many roses," he asked suspiciously.

"It's... it's not what you think. Drake was just trying to make a friendly gesture."

"Wait one damn minute! Is this the same motherfucker you said hurt you so bad in college? The same guy who made you so wary of dating for the longest time?"

"Yes, that's him, but he's trying to make amends about the past. I really think he's changed."

"Oh, so now you're defending him? What's up with that, Alyssa?"

"David, that happened twelve years ago. All I'm saying is I need to let go of all that resentment I've bottled up inside for so long. I have you to thank for helping me move on."

"If you truly have moved on, you would

have dumped those roses in the trash where they belong. Tell me the truth, did something happen with you and him when you were down there?"

"Why are you questioning me like you don't trust me?"

His accusations were valid. I just couldn't bring myself to admit the truth in that moment. The truth would change everything. The truth was I felt David was safe and comfortable. Drake scared me to the core. I was afraid to let myself believe that if I gave my heart completely to him he wouldn't hurt me again.

"By not answering my question, you gave me your answer already."
"David, I just don't have time for an inquisition this morning. We will have to discuss this later."

Stuffing the bag in my hand, he angrily

turned on his heels and headed towards the door.

"David wait! Don't leave like this."

"Nah, I've lost my appetite. I'll give you a call later."

"Are you angry with me, David?"

Stopping in his tracks, he turned to look at me before he reached the door. "Do I have anything to be angry about, Alyssa?"

"That is a question you will have to answer."

"I'm outta here," he said as he opened and slammed the door behind him.

Losing my appetite, as well as suddenly feeling nauseated, I poured the coffee down the drain and trashed the bag containing the cheese Danish.

Chapter 7

My work day was filled with thoughts of David. I felt guilty on so many levels for making him feel as if he was the one in the wrong for questioning me. I had to find a way to make it up to him. Lost in my thoughts, it was a moment before I noticed a student's hand raised to get my attention.

"Miss Darden, I need to use the restroom," Charity said bringing me out of my thoughts.

"Antrinitra, go with Charity to the restroom. Be sure to come straight back and be sure to wash your hands."

Somehow, I made it through my day. I had

never been a person to play with anyone's feelings, and I didn't intend to start. I had to make a choice about my feelings in one way or another, and a choice had to be made and soon. The rest of the work week went by quickly. I hadn't seen David since that awful morning. I tried to talk to him on the phone on numerous occasions. He said he was too busy to take my calls. I knew how busy he could get, although I felt he was using his work as an excuse not to talk to me at all.

Saturday was dreary with rain, but I was determined not to let that put a damper on my day. David worked until twelve on Saturdays, so I thought I would surprise him with an early lunch from his favorite restaurant, *Ravens* on Broadway. I called in and preordered, so all I had to do was pick it up on my way to his bank. I had some making up to do.

Finishing my chores, I bathed and prepared myself for a noon-day tryst with David. I had looked deep and I was ready to commit fully to my relationship with him. I wouldn't put myself in any situation with Drake again that would compromise my relationship with David.

For my tryst, I decided to go all out and put on my purple bra set that I had gotten at Victoria's Secret earlier in the week. The panties were made of see through lace. I moisturized my entire body with my *Sweet Pea* body lotion from Bath and Body Works, as well as sprayed on *Happy* perfume. I decided to wear a red Dolman snapped sleeved shirt and added a pair of black leggings. I stepped into three-inch heels and ran a comb through my slightly curled hair. With only minimum make-up on, I added a glossy shine to my lips and headed out the door.

Ravens was packed, so I was thankful I called ahead with my order. It was early in the day, but I got a bottle of their house wine to go along with our chicken in wine sauce and salads. I was glad David's bank was located across the street from the restaurant. Crossing the street, I entered the lobby of the bank and greeted the security officer as I passed. I made my way over to the elevators and the doors opened as a couple stepped out. Entering the elevator, I punched the button that would carry me to the fifth floor where David's office was located.

I didn't visit him regularly at the bank, but when I did his secretary Jennifer would always greet me with a friendly smile. Jennifer Watson was a nice lady in her early sixties. David always bragged about her proficiency of running the office like a well-oiled machine. When the elevator opened, the first thing I noticed was that she wasn't at her desk. I silently hoped David was still there.

Going over to the door where his name was engraved in a gold plate on the door, I opened the door hoping to pleasantly surprise my man. What I encountered was a surprise of my very own. It was like déjà vu. It was a living nightmare that came to revisit me once again. Only it was broad daylight on a dreary Saturday afternoon. David had his pants down to his ankles and was between a set of thighs that were splayed across his desk. I felt nauseated at the thought that it was Jennifer. She seemed like the motherly type, so I didn't want to believe what I was seeing. I dropped the bags onto the carpeted floor. If it was not for the carpet, the wine bottle would have surly broken.

David stopped mid-stroke when he heard the thud from the bags. Pulling out, he attempted to pull up his slacks to confront the unknown. When he saw me, his green eyes stretched wide in complete shock making his light skin more pronounced than usual. "Alyssa! My God! What are you doing here? I wasn't expecting you."

Not sure how long I could hold the bile attempting to rise in my throat, I barely could get my words out without spewing acid all over the place. "That much is obvious, David! At least now I know what keeps you too busy to receive my phone calls! Is this what keeps you busy twenty four seven?"

I walked farther into the office, so I could tell Jennifer what I thought of her. Then, I realized the woman wasn't Jennifer at all. It was the half white bitch that had shown me no respect when David and I came out of the movie theater a while back. Rachael Simmons.

"Alyssa, give me a moment and I can explain," David said as he came towards me with outstretched hands and a pleading look in his eyes, all the while buckling his belt around his waist.

I had a choice to make. I could show out or I could hold my head up with dignity and walk away with my pride intact. "Save it David. I don't want to hear it. Go back to your little sexcapade. I hope it was well worth it. By the way, enjoy your lunch with your bitch," I said as I exited the office having made the choice to hold my head high. Once again, my heart was shattered.

Chapter 8

Catching a taxi home, I held my tears in until I got inside my apartment. My tears were for me alone and not for the world to see. I especially didn't want David to see not one tear fall for his sorry ass. There I was a grown woman at 32 and I fell for another loser. I would not allow myself to crawl into a fit of depression over him. No, not that time! I was not the same impressionable 20-year-old college student.

The rain was falling in torrents outside. The weather was like my mood, so I didn't want to be alone. I picked up the phone and called Bernadette.

"Hey, what's up?" Bernadette asked on answering.

"I was wondering, if you were busy today?"

"Not really, what's going on with you? You sound like you've been crying."

"I'll tell you when you get here. That is, if you and your man haven't planned anything already."

"Plans or no plans, girl, I am on my way. Give me at least an hour and I'll be on my way."

Hanging up the phone, I went in the bathroom and washed and dried my face. Going into the bedroom, I stepped out of my heels, and stripped out of my clothes. Getting comfortable, I pulled on a pair shorts and a tee. Upon entering the living room, my cell rang on the table where I left it earlier. I saw David's number displayed. I didn't want to answer it, but it was best to get it over and done with.

"Hello David," I said with resignation.

"Alyssa, where are you? Are you home?"

"David, it's not your concern where I am. I answered your call, so you will have no misunderstanding about where we stand. I'll make it simple for you. Don't call me again. When I'm ready to talk, I will call you."

"Alyssa, I'm on my way over."

"What? Didn't you understand a word I said? What do you not understand about don't call. It also goes without saying to not come over. It will be a wasted trip!"

"We need to talk. If we love each other, we can work this out. I really need to see you face to face, baby, so I can explain."

"It's not about what you want or need, David. It's about me, and right now I really need you to leave me the hell alone." I ended the call before I said something in the heat of the moment that I wouldn't be able to take back.

An hour and half later, Bernadette showed up loaded down with all kinds of snacks and not one, but two, bottles of wine.

"What did you do, buy out the store?" I asked her.

"No, but I did raid my pantry," she said as I led her into the living room where she sat her bag on the table, alongside my drying but still pretty roses. "Wow! What's the occasion? What did David do to get in the dog house and buy you so many roses?"

"They aren't from David. Drake sent them."

"What? Girl, you have been holding out on me! Do tell."

"I got them earlier in the week, along with the most beautiful card." Getting up, I went in my bedroom and retrieved the card from the nightstand. Handing the card over to Bernadette, I watched her smile as she began to read it.

"All I can say is this man means business. His words alone would have me falling head over heels for him."

"Well, I think those roses alone is what drove David into another woman's arms today."

"Wait just a damn minute," Bernadette said as she ran to the kitchen and brought back two wine glasses with her. She opened a bottle of the fruity wine and poured some into each glass, before handing one to me and sitting back on the sofa with her own. "Now, tell me everything from the beginning," she said.

Taking a sip from my glass, I told her how David came over the morning, after I received the roses from Drake. I included what led up to our argument and how he angrily left and wouldn't answer my phone calls for days. "I was feeling so guilty for sleeping with Drake that I was willing to overlook his behavior. I was willing to do what I had to just to make things right between us."

"Go on..." Bernadette urged as she pulled her long legs beneath her giving me her undivided attention.

"I made up my mind to try and put what happened with Drake behind me. I was going to put my all into my relationship with David. I wanted to make today special and prove to him how much he meant to me. I got lunch and a bottle of wine, so I could surprise him in his office. But you know what Bernadette?" I asked getting choked up. Rubbing my back in a soothing fashion, she encouraged me to continue without interrupting me. "I was the one in for the surprise. He was having an affair with this woman he used to work with."

"Well, I'm not surprised." Bernadette couldn't hold her tongue any longer. I was surprised she held it that long. "Didn't I tell you before that men do that kind of shit all the time. That's why I'm glad you got it on with Drake when you did. My motto has always been and it's not gonna change anytime soon: Do unto them before they do unto you. That way, you will have less guilt when you're doing your thing."

I couldn't help but shake my head and laugh. That woman always did say the most outrageous things. Then again, maybe if I had her attitude, I wouldn't be so easily hurt.

"Alyssa, I'm going to give you my opinion,

whether you want it or not. You need to call that fine ass Drake up on the phone right now and get you some sexual healing. I bet he would be here so fast, your pretty little head would spin."

"That's why I'm in this mess in the first place. What if I caused David to cheat? Maybe he felt that I had already betrayed him."

"Don't you dare blame yourself for this! Feeling something and knowing it as fact are two different things. Those green eyes didn't see you do shit; therefore, he didn't know a damn thing. You better believe he had sex with that woman, because he couldn't keep it in his damn pants!"

"Doesn't that say the same for me?" I asked. "I didn't control my lust either."

"You know as well as I do that most women are emotional creatures. The majority of the men are not. There had to be deep feelings involved when you were with Drake, because I know the kind of person you are. It wouldn't have happened if there were no feelings. Am I right?" Bernadette asked.

"Yes, but cheating is cheating no matter how you look at it. It's black or white, right or wrong. There are no shades of gray."

"My question to you, Alyssa, is are you married to David? Where is the ring he put on your finger?" Before I could open my mouth to respond, she answered her own question. "Hell no! The only commitment you have is to yourself. Do what makes Alyssa feel good for a change. If opening the door to Drake and giving him a second chance makes you happy, then I say, hell, go for it. Now, hand over that bag of chips. I'm all adviced out for the day," Bernadette said with a grin as she took the bag of chips from me.

"I'm tired of talking myself," I said grabbing the remote and clicking on the television. I hoped there was a good movie on the Lifetime Movie Network.

In a crazy sort of way, Bernadette helped me put things in perspective. She had her quirks, but she was a good and loyal friend.

Chapter 9

The next morning was Sunday, so I went to church. I didn't go as regular as I should, but I knew God loved me regardless. I prayed for God's direction, grace and for mercy in my decisions in the upcoming weeks. After church, I went to a movie and held off going home as long as possible. I was trying to avoid David, in case he decided to drop by. I planned to either change the locks or get him to return my keys.

Breathing a sigh of relief when I found the apartment empty, I grabbed a bite to eat. I showered, grabbed a book from the bookshelf and took it to bed with me. I read until I fell into an exhausted sleep.

It was the Monday morning of the last week of school before summer break. I always planned a little party for the kids on the last day of school as a reward for their hard work throughout the year. I wanted each one to know what an honor it was to have them in my class during the year, and how proud I was to see each one promoted to the next level.

By lunchtime, I could feel a migraine beginning to start and I also felt nauseated. This feeling was not a good combination. It wasn't the first time in the past few days that I had that feeling. I just assumed it was brought on by my stressful situation.

"You don't look good," said Bernadette, as I sat down at the table where she had already started to eat her lunch.

Taking a sip from the sprite I confiscated

from the machine, I took a long sip before I spoke. "Hurry up and eat that tuna sandwich! The smell is really getting next to me."

She looked at me out the side of her eyes. "You're not coming down with that virus that's going around, are you? I really hope you're not, because my cousin had that mess last week." She looked around the room and then whispered, "He had the nerve to bring his sick ass over to my apartment with it and shitted from the time he got there until the time he left."

"Bernadette you are a mess!" I said, laughing even though my head pounded worse. "Trust me, it's just a migraine and sometimes migraines come with nausea."

"If you say so," she said with a doubtful look on her face. "Well, have you heard from David since the last time we talked?"

"No, and I don't expect to. If he follows my

wishes, he'll wait until I call him like I asked him to do."

"We'll have to see how well that works out," Bernadette said as she finished off her sandwich. And truer words were never spoken. At the end of the day, just as Bernadette and I walked out of the school doors, David was leaning against his SUV with his hands in his pockets and his legs crossed at the ankles.

"Just as I thought," Bernadette whispered. "He is not going to wait on the sidelines until you decide what to do about your relationship. Good luck, Alyssa. Unless you want me to stay, I'm out of here."

"Nah, go ahead. I'll see you tomorrow," I said as I went over to confront David. "What the hell are you doing here?" I asked in a low voice.

"I came to give you a ride home," he said as he stepped away from the vehicle.

I slid my school bag from my shoulder and before I realized what he was doing he hurriedly put it on the back seat of his vehicle. He then opened the passenger door and took my elbow and lifted me onto the seat before rushing around to the driver's side. I didn't want to make a scene as my co-workers were leaving the building and getting into their respective cars.

As he slid behind the wheel, he unlooped his navy tie and slung it onto the back seat beside my bag before turning and looking into my angry eyes. "Before you say anything, Alyssa, I want you to know I love you so much it hurts not being able to call you or to see you. I couldn't go another minute of thinking that I would never see you again."

"Take me home, David! I have a migraine the size of the Astrodome and I can't have this conversation with you now. Please, take me home!"

"Of course, I'll take you home, baby. I was hoping you would come over to my house and just relax for a while. I was going to throw a couple of steaks on the grill for us."

Bile began to rise in my throat at the thought of steaks. I wondered what was wrong with me. I felt as queasy as I did when Bernadette was eating her tuna sandwich earlier. "I really need to get home, David," I said again.

He took one look at me and could see that I was in great pain. Starting the vehicle, he drove me home without another word.

"Let me grab your bag. Do you need to see a doctor," he asked as he opened the door for me.

"I'll be fine. I just need a hot bath and a couple of aspirin. Don't worry about me, at all." I hoped he would take the hint and leave, but it fell on deaf ears.

Following closely behind me as I entered my apartment, he pointed me in the direction of the bathroom. "Go on and run your bath water. I will bring you a glass of water to take your aspirin."

I was too sick to argue with him, so I went into the bathroom and adjusted the water temperature to my liking and took the aspirin from my medicine cabinet. In walked David with my glass of water. "Thanks David. Now, I'd appreciate it if you would see yourself out and lock up behind you," I said as I reached for the water and downed the two pills in a hurry. I didn't have the will or the strength to fight with him, but I did want him gone.

"I'm not leaving you in this condition. Get your bath and I will be waiting for you when you come out."

The longer I stood there, the more I realized that I didn't have the energy to make him leave. Closing the door behind him, I stripped and slid into the hot tub of water. Closing my eyes, I tried to shut off the pain throbbing in my temples. I must had dozed off, because I felt myself being lifted out of the tub and laid on the bed. I didn't have the strength to even open my eyes and protest David drying me off. He pulled a nightshirt over my head and slid my arms through the sleeves. He pulled the covers over me and the last thing I remembered before succumbing to sleep, was feeling his lips brush against mine.

Chapter 10

Waking the next morning, I felt like a brand new person. I missed eating lunch and dinner the day before, so the smell of turkey bacon cooking suddenly made me ravenous. Throwing back the covers, I frowned as I looked down at my night shirt. It was funny that I didn't even remember getting ready for bed. Walking into the kitchen, David was standing bare-chested and in boxers at the stove flipping pancakes.

"Good morning, sweetheart. I hope you're hungry. Since you didn't eat anything last night, I figured you needed a good breakfast to keep up your strength."

"Good morning," I said, as I slid into a chair at the table where he had orange juice already poured into two glasses. He put two pancakes and turkey bacon onto my plate and sat it in front of me. My growling stomach let it be known that I was beyond hungry. "Thank you," I said adding maple syrup to my pancakes and digging in like they were going out of style.

He sat down with me at the table with a plate of his own and began eating. I'd forgotten grace, so as David said his I quickly uttered a word of thanks. In no time, I finished my breakfast with a satisfying sigh. I thanked him once again for the delicious breakfast.

"David, why did you stay last night when I asked you to leave?" I said as I looked over at the sofa that had a blanket and pillow, showing evidence of where he had slept.

"Baby, I couldn't leave you when you were too ill to take care of yourself. I would have been less than a man to leave you in a tub of water where you had fell asleep. Besides, you were too weak to lift yourself out of the tub and dress for bed."

"Thank you, for taking care of me. Don't think you are unappreciated or anything, but I'm all better now and you can leave." I got up and gathered the dirty dishes and carried them to the sink. "I have to get ready for work and I know you need to get to the bank too."

"Go get dressed, Alyssa," David said coming up behind me to take over washing the dishes. "I'll see to the dishes and I'll drop you off at the school on my way home to change. I won't give up on what we have that easy, so don't think you can just push me out of your life that easy. We still need to talk."

I didn't want to argue with David that early in the morning, so I left the kitchen without saying another word and readied myself for my workday.

Friday, the last day of school was finally here. My classroom was full of noise and

134

excitement. "Class, please quiet down or principle O'Malley will close down our party. Whoever follows the rules will be given a special gift at the end of the day," I said knowing that would get their attention.

"Yea!" They shouted in unison and then quieted down almost immediately.

I hadn't heard from Drake since I thanked him for the roses. I guessed he had given up on me, after all. That nagging thought followed me through the rest of the day. Those were also the very thoughts that followed me home that evening. Deep in thought I almost passed by my neighbor, Taylor Ashe, who lived across the hall from me, without a word of hello.

"Hi, Alyssa, how are you doing this evening?"

"I'm good, Taylor. Sorry, I didn't see you. I was lost in thought."

"Anything thing I can help you with, just let me know," he said. "Remember, I'm just across the hall."

"Thanks so much, Taylor," I said inserting my key into the lock. "Tell Jennifer that I said hello."

"I sure will," he said as his eyes lit up at the mention of his wife's name.

Later that evening, I was into another episode of NCIS, when my cell began to ring. Weston's number appeared on the I.D.

"I'm glad you called, Wes. You saved me a phone call. I was going to check on you and the girls."

"We are taking one day at a time, Lyssa. I thank God every day for the twins. They are the best part of Denise and me. They are what keeps me grounded and keeps me putting one foot in front of the other."

"They are very precious, Wes. Maybe one day, I'll be able to have that precious joy of having and loving a child of my own."

"You will have all that and more, Alyssa. If Drake had anything to do with it, he would rush you to the altar so fast your head would spin."

"I don't think so, Wes. It's been a while since I heard from him."

"He had to go to Dallas earlier this week. Autumn called with an emergency about their son. I don't quite know all the details yet."

"I hope it's nothing too serious," I said and thought to myself, *so that's why he hadn't called me.*

"What are you going to do since you're on your summer break from the school?"

"You know, Wes, I have been debating that. Usually a couple of friends and I would fly to Florida, and rent a Beach House for two weeks. But, I don't feel like I want to do that this year."

"Alyssa, you mean to tell me that your boyfriend let you out of his sight for that long, and with your friends? I know what kind of trouble a group of women can get into, left that long in a fun city on their own," Wes said chuckling.

"David doesn't have a damn thing to say about what I can or can't do from now on," I said with bitterness lingering on each word.

"Whoa! I must have struck a nerve. I was only joking," Wes defended. "What happened with David to get you this upset?"

"Let's just say my trust in men has once again been misplaced."

"Now Alyssa, please don't place all men in

the same group. All of us are not dogs. In all the years that Denise and I was married, I never once strayed. I can honestly say I wasn't even tempted to. I could have happily lived with that woman a hundred years and I would have been content."

"I'm sorry, Wes," I said feeling contrite, because I knew how special their love was. Weston was in a class all by himself.

"Don't worry about it, Lyssa. By the tone of your voice, I'm assuming David has messed up. Right?"

"Ding, Ding, Ding, your assumptions are correct."

"I'm not going to get you to go into details about what happened, but don't close your heart up again. The right man is out there for you. You just can't give up on love. Love can be most beautiful when you find the one. When you find your other half, you will know it. I had that in Denise. That one woman was my world and, if I had my way, I would choose her all over again even though I would lose her before I was ready."

"You are one of a kind, Weston. I am honored to have you as a friend. You are no David, or Drake for that matter. I will never lump you into the same category as those two ever again."

"I won't speak for David, but Drake was very young and he made a stupid mistake. The combination of being young, high strung and alcohol don't mix. Girls were throwing themselves at him left and right. He rejected them, for he had eyes only for you. That night you caught him with Autumn, he was pretty smashed. I'm not excusing what he did, but I am saying he wouldn't have done it if he hadn't been drinking. He hated how much he hurt you and still regrets it to this day. I'm not going to tell you what to do, Lyssa, but Drake is a good man. When he loves, he loves forever, like me. I'm through preaching to you, but think about what I said."

"I will, Wes. Be sure to give the girls my love." I was at a complete loss of words as I disconnected the call.

Chapter 11

After hanging up the phone with Alyssa, Weston couldn't wait to call Drake.

"Hey, what's up, Wes?" Drake spoke as if he was anticipating Weston's call.

"Man, I just talked to Alyssa and there is trouble with a capital "T" in paradise. If you play your cards right, you just may and I put emphasis on may have a chance to make things right with her."

"What happened? Tell me he didn't put his hands on her."

"No! Cool down man, its nothing like that. I won't go into the details, I just wanted to give you a heads up."

"Good looking out, bruh," said Drake. "I owe you one man."

"Just figure out how to get your woman and your debt will be settled. By the way, how is Drake Jr. doing?"

"He's doing good. He sprung a wrist while skate boarding. Autumn with her histrionics had me thinking he was going to lose a limb."

"That figures," said Weston laughing. "Give me a holla when you make it back to Tiger Town."

"Bet," Drake said ending the call. He sat in his hotel room contemplating calling Alyssa, but didn't want to seem too obvious. He decided to wait a couple of days before calling and making his intentions known in full effect.

To hell with being friends, he wanted more and he wasn't going to continue to pretend otherwise.

***

Saturday afternoon found Bernadette and me doing mall therapy. Nothing could make a woman, young or old, feel better than a new pair of shoes or a sexy new outfit. I was in the dressing room trying on a pair of studded designer jeans in my usual size twelve and I couldn't even zip them. I noticed my clothes had been getting a little snug, but those jeans were ridiculous. I peeked out the dressing room door to get Bernadette's attention. She was looking at some underwear from the sales table. Looking up and spotting me, she came over to see what I wanted. I handed her the pair of size 12 jeans and asked her to get me a size 14.

"Those are too small?" she asked.

"Duh," I said being sarcastic. "Just bring

me a bigger size and I don't want to hear your mouth."

Going and doing my bidding, she brought two pair back, a size 16 along with the size I asked for.

"Girl, I noticed you had gotten thicker in the booty lately, so you better take this size 16 just in case."

Snatching the jeans from her hands, I shut the dressing room door in her face. Turning and looking in the mirror at my booty in my printed briefs, I frowned at the truth of Bernadette's words. The Lord knew I didn't need any more cushion added to the bottom I already had. Trying on the size 14 first I was amazed at the comfortable fit.

"How do your jeans fit?" Bernadette asked on the other side of the door.

Opening the door, I gave her the size 16 back. "You can take those back," I said with a smirk. "The 14 fits just fine. Salads here I come," I muttered while changing back into my clothes.

After paying for our purchases, we left the store with my bigger jeans in tow and headed out the door to Bernadette's red Mazda LX.

"You want to stop and grab a bite to eat before I drop you home?" she asked.

"No, but thanks for hanging out with me today. I will call you one day next week and I'll fix us lunch or dinner, whichever you prefer," I told her.

"Cool," she said. "You know I'm not turning down a meal."

We arrived at my apartment and Bernadette pulled up alongside David's SUV.

"Damn!" I said getting out of the car and gathering my shopping bags.

"Do you want me to come in with you?" she asked.

"No, I need to handle this once and for all. I'll call you later," I said as I waved her off with a smile so that she wouldn't worry. Before I could unlock the door, David opened it with a big smile on his face.

"I've been waiting on you for hours," he said relieving me of my bags.

"A simple phone call would have saved you a trip, David."

"I needed to see you face to face. You have been avoiding my calls."

"The truth is, I need space. I need the time to deal with our situation."

"Alyssa, I'll never be able to apologize enough for what you walked in on in my office.

I wish I could take it back, but I can't. She doesn't mean anything to me, baby," he said sitting the bags on the floor. Taking my hands into his, he squeezed them to express his sincerity.

"What I find really sad and hard to believe is the fact that you had sex with someone that meant absolutely nothing to you. How long have you been seeing her? Was it before we ran into her in the parking lot after leaving the movies?"

"I swear to you, what happened with Rachael wasn't planned. When she worked at the bank, I admit there was an attraction between us that neither of us acted on."

"Basically, what you're telling me is the whole time we've been together you have been lusting over another woman!"

"When we saw her at the movie, that was the first time I had seen her since she left the

148

bank and that is the truth. She came into the bank one day and asked me out to lunch. I wanted to return the favor, so I took her out to lunch last weekend. After lunch, we went back to the office and one thing lead to another and you walked in on the rest. I know this is a hard pill to swallow baby, but we can work through this. Give us a chance," he said bringing a hand to his lips.

"Like I said before, I need time to think," I said looking for understanding in his green eyes that glistened with tears. "I have something for you," I said removing my hands from his.

I went into the bedroom and came back with his things that I had packed in a box for him. "Here," I said as I gave him the box. "Your key to your house is also in the box. Will you kindly return mine?" I held out my hand, palm facing upward.

"Why are you doing this? You know how

much I love you and you are just going to throw us away…just like that."

"David, it looks like we both could use this time apart. I have some issues that I need to work out too, so I will not lay all the blame at your feet. I honestly think the time apart will do us both good."

"I am not going to agree with you on that, Alyssa! Being apart in some instances does not make the heart grow fonder. We need to stay together and work through this. I know I was in the wrong and I promise you I will fix this, if you give me the chance."

"Whether you will admit it or not, maybe you need to see if there is more going on between you and Rachael than you are willing to admit."

"Is there someone you want to be with, Alyssa? Where is all this coming from?"

"Just please hand over the key," I said ignoring his question.

He took the key from his key ring and placed it in my hand. I knew I was wrong for not coming clean about my own infidelity with Drake. But, what good would it have done to hurt David in the same way he had hurt me? Not one bit of good according to my own reasoning.

"When you want me, you know where to find me. Just don't wait too long," he said on his way out the door.

Chapter 12

What is wrong with me? I thought as the ringing phone woke me from a sound sleep on Sunday morning. Lately, all I wanted to do was sleep. Glancing at the clock beside my bed, I wondered who could be calling at 8 a.m. on a Sunday.

"Hello," I said sleepily into the phone.

"Alyssa, it's me Drake." The sound of his voice made me sit up in bed wide awake. "I'm sorry I woke you, but I couldn't go any longer without hearing your voice."

"Don't be sorry. Actually, I'm glad you

152

called," I said smiling. "I wanted to ask you how was Drake Jr.? Wes told me he had some kind of accident."

"He's going to be fine. He sprung his wrist skate boarding."

"Thank God it wasn't anything worse."

"His mom had me thinking he had broken almost every bone in his body."

"I'm glad to hear that he will be okay," I said thinking how Autumn probably hadn't changed in all the years since college. She was probably the same conniving little thing she'd always been.

"Thank you, baby." His voice broke into my musing. "What I want to know is how are you doing, Lyssa?"

"I'm okay," I said as I settled back onto my pillows.

"I want you to be doing a lot better than just okay. I want to see you. No, let me change that. I need to see you, baby. Do you think we can make that happen?"

I wanted to see him in the worst way possible. With David out of the picture, there was nothing to stop me. "What did you have in mind?" I asked.

"Since you have the summer at your disposal, I was wondering could you come here. Before you answer that, I want you to know that my house is big and you could have your own room, if that's your desire. We can get to know each other again and we can take it slow, with no pressure."

"I'll come, Drake."

"You've just made my day."

"When do you want me there?" I asked.

154

"Right now isn't soon enough for me, but let me check any available flights and times. I'll get back with you as soon as I arrange everything. All you have to do is pack."

"Okay, I just hope I won't regret this."

"Oh, you won't, trust me."

After disconnecting the call with Drake, I slid deeper under my comforter. I smiled as I waited for him to call me back with my flight information.

Within minutes, he called to tell me my ticket would be waiting on me at JFK and he would be waiting on me at the Hartsfield, when I landed on Tuesday in Atlanta. I declined his offer to send a car to take me to the airport. Bernadette insisted on taking me herself. I gave her a key to my apartment to keep a check on the place, while I was away. I also left her with Drake's address and phone numbers so she would have all the information, if she needed it for any reason.

When I landed in the ATL on Tuesday evening, Drake was waiting on me just as he promised. Dressed in Polo Jeans and a navy polo shirt that emphasized his broad chest and muscular arms, he looked so good my mouth began to water. My mind thought of the many delicious things I could do with him. Noticing that his big feet were encased in soft leather Sperrys, I admired his style. From his head to his feet, I couldn't get enough of looking at him. His dark chocolate skin and low cut wavy hair were a deadly combination with those sexy hazel eyes. I knew I wouldn't stand a chance of fighting my attraction to him. If I were to be completely honest with myself, I didn't really want to.

"Alyssa, I'm so glad to see you," he said as his eyes roamed from my head to my toes. "You look beautiful," he said admiring my yellow shirtwaist dress that was belted at the waist.

My feet were freshly pedicured and encased in strappy sandals. Pulling me to him, he kissed me fully on my strawberry flavored glossed lips, not caring that we were surrounded by people in the crowded airport. "I needed that more than you'll ever know, baby," he muttered against lips that yearned for more of his kiss.

Breaking our contact, he gathered my bags and led me out the door to his black Escalade that he left waiting at curbside. Opening the passenger door for me to get in, he pecked me on my lips before placing my bags in the back and getting behind the wheel.

"Thank you for picking me up," I said suddenly at a loss for words. My heart was beating so fast I had to take deep breaths to control it. The scent of his musky cologne wasn't helping any.

"Baby, don't thank me. I thank you for coming and giving me a chance to prove myself to you, again. I love you even more for giving up your summer and taking this leap of faith," he said as he pulled into the busy traffic.

Staring at his profile as he drove, I pleaded my case. "Drake, I am taking a leap of faith, so please don't hurt me again. I don't know if I'll be able to take it if you hurt me for a second time."

Momentarily taking his eyes off the road as he stopped for a traffic light, he took his right hand from the steering wheel and lifted my left hand to his lips and kissed it. "I will promise you that I will not hurt you in that way again. We will have our disagreements as you will in any relationship. But, I am not that young boy anymore who can't control his hormones. I'm a man who won't throw away the best thing that ever happen to him for anything."

"You should tell David how a grown man should be able to control his hormones," I said before thinking how much of a hypocrite I was.

I had done the same thing with Drake that David had done with Rachael. "I'm sorry. I didn't mean for that to come out. I don't want the time that we have together to be a reflection on what happened between David and I. So will you just forget I said that?"

Giving my hand another reassuring squeeze, he said, "It's forgotten until you bring it back up. I want you to be able to talk to me about anything, Alyssa. I will be there for you in any capacity that you need me to be."

"Thank you, Drake. I'll keep that in mind," I said returning my eyes to the scenery as we headed toward Auburn.

ASK ME AGAIN

Chapter 13

On arrival to his War Eagle Drive Estate, I was speechless. His house was much bigger than anything I was used to. Going around the winding driveway with its lush green lawn and shrubbery on both sides, there were plenty of trees to provide shade on long hot summer days.

"Your home is beautiful," I said as he drove into a garage that could hold at least four cars. I knew if it was that beautiful on the outside it had to be even more beautiful on the inside.

"Thanks baby. Think of this as your home too. Nothing that I have is off limits when it comes to you," he said as he lowered the garage doors with push of a button from the console.

Opening his car door, he got out and opened my door before taking my bags from the back. I followed through a side door that led into a big and elegant kitchen that would make any Food Network chef proud. Following him through the kitchen, I caught a glimpse of a dining room that would be just perfect for large family gatherings. The living room was spacious, with beautiful African art work gracing the walls.

Leading me toward the spiral stairway, he said, "The bedrooms are up the stairs. As promised, you will have your own bedroom." He stopped at the third door on the left and sat the luggage down as he opened the door for me to enter. "I hope you like it. I had it freshly painted just for you," he said as I took in the beautiful lavender walls trimmed in white.

He placed my luggage on the floor by the Queen sized bed, which was embellished with a lavender trimmed in white Tiffany bedding set. The many accent pillows added a romantic look.

"The room is lovely," I said turning to face him. I felt nervous that we were truly alone in that bedroom.

"Your bath is through that door." He nodded towards a closed door across the room. "You also have plenty of closet space." He motioned toward the other door.

"Thank you, Drake. This room has everything that I will need and more," I said as I looked at the giant flat screen plasma on the wall.

"Take your time and unpack, refresh yourself and I'll fire up the grill and put on the steaks that I left marinating in the fridge. You got to be hungry after your flight. Come on down, when you're ready," Drake said looking into my eyes as if he wanted to say more, before he turned and left but decided against it.

I made quick work of unpacking my clothes, placing fresh undies on the bed along with shorts and a tee shirt. I entered the bathroom noticing every feminine product I needed was already in stock in the cabinets. I was touched by Drake's thoughtfulness and generosity. After shedding my clothes, I adjusted the water temperature and stepped into the shower to wash away my tiredness with the bath sponge and citrus body wash that was left for me to use. The scent of the body wash revived me as the streaming water washed away the suds from my body. Stepping from the shower, I grabbed a big fluffy towel to dry my body. Slathering the citrus body lotion onto my slightly damp body, I rubbed it in from head to toe. The lotion left my skin soft and supple to the touch. I finished dressing and slid my feet into sandals before deciding to

164

look for Drake.

I entered the kitchen expecting to find Drake. Instead, I saw him through the sliding glass doors that led to the patio. Shirtless with jeans hanging low on his hips, I licked my lips wanting to devour him where he stood. My appetite was bigger than the juicy steaks he was turning on the grill.

"Hey baby," he said motioning for me to come out and join him.

"What can I do to help?" I asked going over to stand beside him. Looking me up and down with the same hungry look I had given him earlier, his eyes stayed longer on my thick bare thighs.

"Go on over and take a seat," he said motioning toward cushioned chairs and a table laid out with plates, glasses and cutlery.

"Are you sure you don't need any help?"

"I'm very sure," he said giving my ass a lingering stare as I turned and did as he instructed. The sexual tension was so thick you could cut it with a knife.

I was in for the fight of my life, because I didn't want to give in to the many emotions I was feeling. We needed to take things slow and get to know each other again, without adding sex to the equation. I needed to keep a clear head and making love to Drake would only confuse me more. My head was logical, my heart and body were not. Time would tell which would win.

Noticing the obvious bulge in his jeans wasn't helping any. My eyes had a will of their own as they roamed over his six pack hard abs and strong muscular arms. Next, my eyes collided with his hazel gaze and the unbridled lust was evident.

"Alyssa, if you keep looking at me like that,

we will have to forget dinner."

"I... I'm not looking at you. I was just wondering how long the steaks would be. I'm starving."

"Okay," he said with a knowing smile. "Do me a favor and grab the salad out of the fridge and we can eat."

Almost running into the kitchen to get away from his knowing look, I opened the fridge and leaned in hoping the cool air would cool down my heated body. Taking the salad bowl from the fridge, I noticed a pitcher of iced tea and grabbed that too. Turning, I almost dropped the salad bowl I was balancing in one hand. "Don't sneak up on me like that!" I gasped.

"I didn't mean to scare you," he said taking the salad bowl from my hand. "I was coming to grab the iced tea, but I see you were bringing it already. Come on, let's eat while the steaks are warm," he said as he took my free arm and ushered me back out the door.

The steaks were seasoned to perfection. I wasn't a big steak eater, but it melted in my mouth like butter.

"Dinner was absolutely delicious, but I won't have you waiting on me hand and foot, while I'm here."

"That's cool," Drake said. "Because, you can have the cooking if that's what you want."

"I wouldn't go that far, but we can share the cooking," I said with a wink and smile.

"Whatever you want, Alyssa... whatever you want you got it," he said with double meaning.

I took a deep breath to control my body's response and heard voices coming towards us. Weston came into view immediately followed by Alisha and Alexis. "Hi Aunt Alyssa!" They screamed in unison as they ran and bombarded me with hugs and kisses.

"What about me?" Drake said standing up.

"Aww Uncle Drake, we see you all the time," Alisha said as they went to hug him too.

"Oh, so it's like that, huh?" He pretended to be hurt.

"Nooooo. You know how much we love you, Uncle Drake," Alisha spoke up this time in a serious tone belying her youthfulness.

"I'm just teasing you, squirts," he said tickling her until she cried.

"Uncle!"

"I had to come and see my favorite friend," Weston said as I stood to give him a hug. "Actually after Lexi and Lisha found out you were here, they wouldn't take no for an answer until I brought them to see you. We should have called first," Weston said with a sheepish grin.

"Man you know you and the girls never need an invitation to come over here, so don't pretend that you do. You know how we do it," Drake said while pulling Alisha's ponytail. "Are you guys hungry?"

"Nah man, we just came from eating pizza, so we're cool."

I stood and began to clear the table while Drake and Weston talked.

"I'll help you with the dishes," Alisha said as she gathered the remaining dishes and followed me into the kitchen.

"I'll help too," Alexis said bringing in the salad bowl.

Chapter 14

"Are you and Uncle Drake dating?" Alisha asked as I put the last dish into the dishwasher.

Before I could answer her question, Alexis said, "Mommy talked about you all the time. She said you and her were joined at the hip. She said when you were in college, you loved Uncle Drake as much as she loved daddy."

Smiling at the memory of Denise, I wasn't surprised she confided that information in her beautiful daughters. Looking into their eyes was like having Denise right there with me. In that moment, I wondered what it would have been like if Drake and I had married when he asked me. How many kids would we have had? "It's kind of complicated, but your mom was right. Drake and I were very much in love."

"Why didn't you marry him like mommy married daddy?" Alexis persisted.

"It just didn't work out that way," I answered knowing they were too young to understand the complications that come with adulthood situations. "Sometimes things happen in a relationship, and although you may still love that person, you just have to let them go."

"Is that why Uncle Drake married that mean Miss Autumn?" Alexis piped in.

"Ooooh, I'ma tell daddy," Alisha said. "Daddy said to never call her mean, because if Drake Jr. heard us call his mom mean it would make him sad."

172

"Well, your dad is right. It's not right to call her mean. Let's just keep it between us this time, Alisha. I'm sure your sister will remember not to say it again."

"I'll remember, I promise," she said lisping through her missing front tooth. "Mommy also said that Uncle Drake loved you with passion?"

Widening my eyes, I couldn't believe Denise. "What else did your mom say?" I asked.

"She said he loved his baby too. That's why he married Miss Autumn so that his baby would have a daddy like our daddy."

Denise! If you were here you would really have some explaining to do. How in God's name did she fix her mouth to tell her babies something like that? Looking at them, I explained, "Your mom was right. When you have a responsibility you should take care of it.

173

A child, especially a baby, needs both parents, if it's at all possible. You girls are so very smart. I just know that your mom is looking down on you both saying how proud she is of you." As Weston and Drake entered the kitchen, they found me hugging both girls in each arm.

"Come on girls. Let's make a move," Wes said coming over to give me another hug.

"Ahhh daddy! Why do we have to leave so soon?" Alisha whined.

"Because, I said so squirt. Now, say your goodbyes and let's go," he said leading them out of the door.

"I'll see you soon. Maybe we can have a girls' day out," I said bringing the desired smiles to their faces. Closing the door behind them, I turned and found Drake watching me. "Why are you staring at me like that?"

"I was just thinking how great of a mother you would be. If I hadn't messed up, we could have had a couple of kids of our own by now."

"You already have a beautiful son. I noticed the numerous photos of him scattered throughout the house. He looks just like you; he even has your hazel eyes," I said as he came closer to me with a look of intent.

"Thank you, sweetheart. That means a lot coming from you."

"Your son is an innocent child. I don't hate him, no matter the circumstance. I don't even hate his mother anymore, although I could never be her friend. I had to let go of all that anger, because it was eating me alive. I stayed bitter for a long time. I can thank David for helping me through that," I said truthfully as I looked into his eyes. "He opened my heart up to the possibility of love again." I knew he didn't like the thought of me loving David, but I didn't want our relationship to start with me lying about my feelings for David.

"What about me? Have you opened your heart enough to forgive me too?" Drake asked.

I rubbed my hand along his strong jaw line feeling his evening stubble as I looked into the warmth of his hazel eyes and told him what was in my heart.

"Even in the midst of all my anger, I have never hated you. I told you I hated you, because I wanted you to feel the same pain I felt at the time. The truth was I loved you so much it hurt. When I found out that Autumn was pregnant and you had married her, it felt like someone had died. Autumn had everything that was supposed to have been for me. I was supposed to be the one carrying your child."

"Lyssa, I never stopped loving you. I married her for the sake of my child and for my child alone. I know I wasn't fair to Autumn carrying another woman in my heart. We never really had a chance. I could never see her for you. To be honest, I even brought you into our bedroom. You have to know that if it had been you I married, child or no child, I would never had let you go."

"Then wasn't our time Drake. There was no way I could marry you back then. I needed the time to grow and be the independent woman I am today. In a way, I have you to thank for me having to leave this small town after college. Dad was gone, you were gone, and Denise had Weston. Going to New York, helped me forget. I was so busy learning a new way of life that I didn't have time to feel sorry for myself. I either had to sink or swim and I chose to swim."

"Baby, I'm proud of what you accomplished. I would never have tried to hold you back. You were my biggest cheerleader, during my time on the college team. I missed you like hell when I turned pro. Eventually, I convinced myself that you were better off without me.

After I got hurt, I had to figure out what I wanted to do after football. I'm so glad I had my degree in business to fall back on. It helps me a lot in the running of the A & D Community Centers. So, I understand what it means to accomplish your dreams baby. All I ask is that from now on you let me be a part of your dreams," Drake said before pulling me into his arms. First kissing the top of my head, he trailed light kisses down my cheek until he reached my waiting lips. He nipped my lips open with his teeth to receive his exploring tongue.

Meeting his tongue with a ferocity of my own, I knew I was lost once again in the building fire budding in my core. My nipples pressed hard against his chest matching the hardness of his erection that I felt through his jeans. "Drake, we can't do this," I said between his feverish kisses.

"Why can't we, Lyssa? We're both consenting adults and we're not strangers, by any means."

When he delved his head to bite gently at a sensitive spot on my neck, I clung to him trying to get closer as he pressed my hips hard against his arousal. As he palmed my ass, I writhed against him as the pool of wetness in my panties became more pronounced.

"I have got to have you now, Lyssa," he said as he unzipped and pushed down my shorts and panties in one swoop. I stepped out of my shorts as Drake unzipped and pulled down his jeans. He lifted me and I wrapped my thick legs around his trim waist. Kissing me as we backed into the nearest wall, I was still amazed by his huge arousal. "Baby, I can't go slow this time. I want you too damn bad. Are you ready for me?"

Before I could answer, he entered me entirely. My wet canal received and clamped down on him like a snug glove.

"Umpf, umpf..." The guttural sounds he made deep in his throat had me moaning in orgasmic pleasure. As he rammed into me, my juices released around his rod. I could feel my juices running down the sides of my thighs as he continued to glide in and out of my contracting pussy. "Ahh Ahh... Shit Alyssa you are so damn hot! Fuck, I'm fixing to cum baby. Cum with me again," he said as he bit my hard nipple through my tee shirt.

Just as he ordered, I came as I felt his hot seed splatter against my walls. Sliding down his sweaty body, weak at the knees, he supported me with an arm around my voluptuous waist.

"Let's take this upstairs," he said as he pulled me along behind him.

I couldn't help but admire the view as I followed behind him. Pulling me to his masculine bedroom, he bypassed the bed and led me into a full bath consisting of a Jacuzzi tub, a double walk-in shower and double sinks.

Opening the doors of the shower, he adjusted the temperature and finished undressing me before pulling me into the shower with him. Being sure not to wet my hair, he wet a sponge and added an ample amount of body wash. With his back to the shower to block most of the water from hitting me, he began to wash my front, starting at my neck and shoulders. Washing my already sensitive breasts had me biting my lip and closing my eyes as the sensation began to build once again between my thighs. Not one place was left untouched when he rinsed all the suds from my body.

Taking the sponge from him, I added the body wash and washed his body as thoroughly as he had washed mines but saving the best for last. I held his hardness in my hand admiring his length and width before I soaped up and washed him with my hands. He made a hissing sound between his teeth that let me know he was affected by my ministrations.

"You need to stop. You don't know what

you're doing to me."

"I think I do," I said as I rinsed him, went down on my knees, and enveloped him into my moist, hot mouth.

Drake reared back in surprise as I suctioned him deeper, almost gagging as he hit the back of my throat. I hoped I would please him, as that was my first time attempting that type of pleasure. I knew I wouldn't be able to take in his full length since he was half way in and he was already hitting the back of my throat. Moaning in surrender, he placed his hands on my head and moved in sync with my mouth.

Drawing back, I flicked my tongue across the head, still stroking him with both hands. As I tongued the tip of his sensitive head, he began to moan my name over and over. Feeling more confident in my efforts, I ran my tongue up and down his shaft even lightly licking his balls. When I licked under his balls, he laid back on the shower wall as if he needed something solid to help him stand. He became even harder as I enveloped him back into my mouth. I sucked harder as his moans urged me on. When I ran my tongue along the rim of his head, he tried to pull me up. I sucked harder and faster as he came hard into my mouth and I swallowed every drop of his sweet cum like a pro.

"Damn Alyssa," he said as he pulled me up. "You got me all whipped and shit." Reaching around me, he cut off the shower. Taking two large towels from a closet, he wrapped me in one and himself in the other.

Taking a bottle of body oil, he led me over to his king-sized bed that was already turned down. Pushing me face down onto the bed, he took the oil and rubbed it all over my body, paying close attention as he squeezed and rubbed my buttocks in a circular motion.

Closing my eyes in pure pleasure, I moaned

when his hands were replaced with soft biting kisses as he spread my butt cheeks and softly blew. Flipping me onto my back, I was totally at his mercy and manipulation as he oiled my front with the same care that he showed to my backside. Squeezing my supple breasts, he took a nipple into his mouth, which caused me to undulate my hips wanting relief from the pressure building inside of me.

"Alyssa, you are like a drug to me," he muttered as he trailed delicious kisses down my body. He stopped at the heat between my thighs and exhaled my essence. "You're so wet baby," he said as he draped one leg onto his wide shoulder.

Spreading me open, I was vulnerable to the rough swipe of his tongue. Grabbing his head, I began to grind against his mouth as he continued to love me with his tongue and mouth. Letting go with a scream, I came with a gush as he lapped up my juices like nectar. Before I could fully recover, Drake entered me swift and hard. Wrapping my legs around his waist, I met him stroke for stroke.

Capturing my lips, he plunged his tongue into my mouth and French kissed me causing my walls to clamp down on his hardness, as yet another orgasm impaled upon me with such force that it caused Drake to come a heartbeat later. Drake pulled the sheet over our bodies and took me into his arms as we fell into an exhausted sleep.

Chapter 15

The next morning, I awakened to the sun peeking through the drapes. Turning over and reaching for Drake, much to my disappointment, I found an empty space. Before I could get out of bed, he opened the bedroom door balancing a tray in one hand.

"Good morning beautiful," he said as I noticed he had put on pajama bottoms, which left me at a disadvantage of being totally naked beneath the sheets.

"Good morning," I returned and smiled as he set the tray on the bed in front of me. I sat up in bed and fluffed the pillows. "You didn't have to do this," I said as he uncovered my plate and the smell of bacon accosted my nostrils. There were softly scrambled eggs with grits on the side, as well. I tried to hold my smile in place as I swallowed hard and tried hard not to be nauseated.

"What's wrong, baby?" Drake asked noticing my expression.

Before I could answer, the nausea feeling took control and I pushed the tray aside and hurried to the bathroom. Heaving, I emptied everything from the night before and beyond, it seemed, into the toilet.

Drake entered the bathroom and took a bath cloth from the closet. He wet the cloth with cool water before bending and placing the cloth on the back of my neck. He rubbed my back as I continued to dry heave with nothing left to come up. When I finished, he flushed the toilet and helped me to my feet.

"I'm sorry," I said feeling embarrassed for getting sick in front of him.

"Don't apologize for being sick. You may have picked up a bug or ate something that disagreed with your stomach."

"Maybe," I said as I thought about the frequent upset stomach episodes I had been getting along with the migraines. I rinsed my mouth at the sink, and Drake took a new toothbrush out of the cabinet and gave it to me.

"Thanks. If you don't mind, I'd like to get cleaned up and I'm so sorry about the breakfast. I know you went to a lot of trouble making it and I appreciate it."

"No problem, baby. I'll be downstairs when you get ready, and don't worry about the bed or anything. The cleaning service is due today." Picking up the tray of uneaten food, Drake left me to get showered and dressed.

Before going downstairs, I went into the bedroom that I didn't sleep in and took my cell from my purse to call Bernadette.

"Hey girl," she said answering the phone. "What happened to calling me once you landed safely?"

"Sorry about that, but as you see I landed safely with no problems whatsoever. Drake was waiting for me at the airport as promised."

"I bet that wasn't all he was waiting on," she said with a giggle.

"Girl you are too much." I laughed with her and talked a few more minutes before saying goodbye.

Drake had just finished cleaning the kitchen when I found him. Walking up behind him, I wrapped my arms around his waist. Turning into my embrace, he gave me a lingering good morning kiss. "Are you feeling better, baby?" he asked as he nuzzled the side of my neck. "Mmmm, you smell so good."

"Much better and feeling better all the time," I said with a suggestive arch to my brow.

"Keep it up and you will be back in bed. Since you're all fresh and clean, I'm going to run on up and shower."

"I'm not going anywhere, so take your time," I said as I watched his taut butt walk out of the kitchen.

The ringing of the phone on the kitchen wall startled me. I waited a while before answering it. I waited to see if Drake would grab the extension in his room. *Maybe he is in the shower,* I thought as it continued to ring, so I decided to answer.

"Hello, Peterson res..."

Before I could utter another word, the caller asked, "Who is this?"

"Excuse me," I said, not believing the audacity of the female caller's attitude.

"I said Who-The-Hell-Is-This?" she said slowly as if I had just come off the short bus. "Never mind. Just put Drake on the phone."

"Drake is busy right now," I said in my most pleasant voice, when I really wanted to give the bitchy woman a piece of my mind, whoever she was. Instead, I added extra syrup to my voice. "May I take a message?"

"Tell Drake to call his wife and don't have me waiting," she said before slamming the phone down so hard it left a loud buzzing tone in my ear.

How could I forget her voice? It was Autumn Blake Peterson! And, she was still a bitch with a capital B. Time had not changed her one bit. Where in the hell did she get off still calling herself his wife? I was still contemplating her words when Drake came into the family room where I was flipping through a magazine.

"I wondered where you had gone off too," he said sitting down beside me.

Laying the magazine onto the table, I turned to him and looked into his eyes to note his reaction. "Your wife called, while you were in the shower."

"Don't you mean my ex-wife?" he said with emphasis arching his left brow.

"I'm just passing along the message exactly as it was given," I said with a relieved smile. "Oh yeah, and she said don't keep her waiting."

Shaking his head in bemusement, he pulled me onto his lap. "That is one woman that is full of drama," he said before lowering his head and kissing me with so much tenderness it put Autumn into the furthest recess of my mind.

Chapter 16

I had been so caught up in my life's drama that I hadn't realized the period I missed the month before. The morning sickness and being lightheaded on occasion were beginning to make sense. As I thought back to the evening after Denise's funeral when I let Drake follow me back to my hotel, I remembered we had not used protection.

When Drake left to go to the community center to catch up on some paper work, he promised he would only be gone for a couple of hours. Looking at the keys he left for me to drive his Mercedes, I grabbed the keys and my purse and drove to the nearest CVS pharmacy.

Once at the store, I went straight to the home pregnancy tests and purchased three different kinds of test. I didn't want to get upset for nothing and I figured three tests would prove if I was or wasn't pregnant. Once home, I headed straight to my bedroom, only taking enough time to lay down my purse before going into the bathroom. Following the test's directions, I awaited the required amount of time, biting my nails the whole time.

Finally getting the nerve, I looked at one of the tests. My worse fear was confirmed as the other two confirmed the same positive results. *Fuck!* How was I going to handle this? True, I wanted kids but I had no plans of becoming an unwed mother, even at my age. A thirty four year old woman such as myself should know better than to get in that kind of situation. I had kids looking at me to set a better example. Being unmarried and pregnant was not the kind of example I wanted to set for my second graders. Most of the kids learned about the birds and the bees at an early age, so there would be no sugar coating my pregnancy.

Oh my God! How was I going to tell Drake? Maybe he wouldn't believe the baby was his? All those thoughts went through my head as I sat on the closed toilet seat. I had been with David on multiple occasions after Drake, but we used protection every time. There was no doubt in my mind that it was Drake's baby. Dumping the empty boxes into the trash, I disposed of all the test strips except one and carried it with me into the bedroom. I laid it on the nightstand as tears coursed down my cheeks. Kicking off my shoes, I laid across the bed and closed my eyes. As tiredness overcame me, I fell asleep.

Opening my eyes after what seemed like a couple of hours, I found Drake laying on his side staring intently at me as I slept. Before I could say a word, he took me into his arms and gave me the sweetest kiss.

"What time is it?" I asked when I could

finally speak.

"It's almost six thirty," he said glancing at his watch.

"Wow! I've been sleeping for a while," I said as I sat up and glanced at the evidence I left on the nightstand.

"When I first got home, I called out to you and I didn't get an answer, so I went to my bedroom hoping you were there waiting for me, but you weren't there. I decided to check in here before going back downstairs and here you were sleeping so sound that I didn't want to wake you. I enjoyed watching you sleep like a beautiful angel," he said as he brushed a wisp of hair out of my face. "Don't you have something you want to tell me?"

"I don't have to Drake. I'm sure you already saw the evidence."

"Baby," he said smiling. "You've made me

the happiest man on God's green earth."

"Why aren't you asking me is the baby yours?"

"Have you had unprotected sex with anyone besides me?"

"No, I haven't and it was very foolish of me to have it with you."

"It happened and there is no time for regrets now. We have a beautiful baby we have to prepare for. I felt we had made a baby that night. Yes!" he said pumping his arm as if he ran a touchdown. "We need to get you a doctor's appointment as soon as possible. Let me pull some strings and see what I can do," he said as he walked out of the room. The next day, I was sitting in Dr. Faye Washington's office. She had her own OB/GYN practice in the Auburn Medical Park and her husband, Alvin, was a good friend of Drake's.

After signing in, I was given a medical sheet on a clipboard to fill out with all my information on it. Thanking the receptionist, I took a seat beside Drake who hadn't stopped smiling since he found out I was pregnant.

"Baby, you don't have to worry about anything," he said as I filled out the sheet. "I will pay all your expenses that the insurance doesn't pay."

"Can we discuss that later, Drake?"

"What is there to discuss? I am going to take care of my responsibilities and that includes you and my baby. You can get used to that," he said in a matter of fact tone.

Letting the subject drop, I returned the clipboard with the filled out information, along with my insurance card, to the receptionist. After making a copy of my insurance card, she promptly handed it back to me with a smile and promised it wouldn't be long before I would be called back. Looking around the waiting room, I noticed one woman who looked like she was about to drop her load at any given time. Taking a hold of my hand and holding it between his, Drake soothed my nerves with his calming presence.

"It will be okay Alyssa. I'm going to be with you every step of the way, for you and our baby. We are in this together," he said bringing my hand to his lips and softly kissing it.

It didn't matter that the majority of the women there were pregnant. They were still checking out Drake's physique and handsomeness and looking on wistfully as if they wished he was their man giving them the attention that he was giving to me.

"Alyssa Darden," the nurse called. "You may come on back."

Drake was only a step behind me as we

followed the nurse to exam room #5.

"I'm Stephanie and I need you to go across the hall to the restroom and leave a urine sample and put your name on the cup. When you return, put this gown on and be sure to leave the opening in the front," she said not taking her eyes off Drake as she smiled showing all her teeth.

As I looked at the blue-eyed blond-headed nurse, I thought some women were just scandalous. "Thank you," I said gaining her attention. She looked at me as if she had forgotten that I was in the room.

"You're welcome and the doctor will be with you shortly." She turned and left the room with an extra twist in her scrub-clad hips.

"What?" Drake asked as I looked at him to see his reaction to Nurse Stephanie's obvious flirtations.

"Nothing," I said as I went across the hall to leave a urine sample as the nurse instructed. Going behind the curtain, I stripped and put on the gown as Drake sat patiently in a chair.

"I've seen all of you. There is no need for you to undress behind the curtain," he said as I sat on the table.

"You don't have to stay for the examination. You can wait in the waiting room," I said suddenly feeling nervous. "I will let you know what the doctor says."

Looking at me as if I had lost my mind, he said, "Don't think I'm going to miss a moment of this experience with you. I'm going to be there from start to finish, so let that be the end of this silly discussion," he said in all seriousness. Before I could respond, there was a tap on the door and Dr. Washington entered with a big friendly smile.

"Drake it's good to see you again," she said including us both in her gaze and smile.

He rose and greeted her with a kiss to her cheek. "Good to see you too, Faye! It's been a while. Thank you, so much for taking the time out your busy schedule to see Alyssa."

"It wasn't a problem," she said reaching to shake my hand. "Anything to help out an old friend. Miss Darden, your urine sample did confirm that you are indeed pregnant. The ultrasound will tell how far along you are and your blood work will have to be done. If you will lie back, we will get this exam underway and I will make it as comfortable for you as possible.

"Now, that wasn't too bad," Dr. Washington said as she squeezed the clear cold gel on my belly five minutes later. "Everything looks good. The baby's heartbeat is steady and strong. It's too early to tell the sex of your baby, but it looks like you're about seven weeks along."

Hearing the baby's heartbeat for the first time made everything more real and clearer to me. For the first time in my adult life, it wasn't going to be just me anymore. Feeling Drake's eyes on me, I looked into his glassy hazel eyes as he stood beside me taking my hand and bringing it to his lips. He kissed the center of my palm and closed my hand as if not to let the kiss escape.

Lost in our thoughts, the doctor's voice brought us back to the exam. "I will have the nurse give you a picture of your baby from the ultrasound."

"Thank you doctor," we both said in unison never taking our eyes off each other.

Chapter 17

"I hope you aren't too tired," Drake asked as we were eating a scrumptious but healthy lunch after leaving the doctor's office.

"No, I'm not. What's up?"

"I wanted to take you by the community center while we were out, if you're up to it."

"I would love to see your dream in motion, Drake. I remember when we were in college, and how you use to talk about one day opening a place where kids would have a place to go and have positive mentors in their lives who would help them to achieve their goals. I am so glad you were able to make your dream a reality and, in living out your dream, you are helping others at the same time."

"Thank you, baby, but I'm doing no more

204

than you are. Teaching is an admirable profession and any child is lucky to have you as a teacher. They will be even more blessed to have you for a mother."

Blushing, I looked down at my almost empty plate and felt Drake's finger lift my chin. He stared deeply into my eyes. "I love you woman. Don't you know that I never stopped?"

"I love you too, Drake," I said as a tear seeped from my eye.

Catching my tear on a fingertip, Drake wiped it away. "No time for tears. I want you to be happy." Throwing several bills on the table, he stood and pulled me into his arms and kissed me, not caring who was watching.

Once we reached the A & D Community Center, he gave me a tour and introduced me to some of his staff that were there. Everyone was friendly and seemed to truly care about the kids that were entrusted in their care.

"Hey Mr. D!" Called a boy that looked to be about seventeen. He came up and gave Drake a pound.

"Treveon, this is Miss Alyssa Darden, someone that is special to me. Alyssa this is Treveon Carter, the next Michael Jordan."

"Nice to meet you, Miss Alyssa. You are pretty. If I were older, Mr. D wouldn't have a chance."

"Boy, you got jokes, huh? Let's see how many jokes you got the next time I see you on the court," Drake said with a laugh as Treveon ran back to his game.

"He is a sweetheart. Are all the kids like him?"

"Unfortunately, no. Some of these kids come from broken homes and have serious problems. For some, this is a place of refuge and escape. Come on, I'll show you my office and then I'll take you home so you can get off of your feet."

"Drake, I'm pregnant, not an invalid," I said as we walked to his office. "I can't believe you still have this picture of us." I picked up the same picture I broke while leaving his college dorm in a rush after finding him and Autumn together. It had been replaced in a different frame. I looked at our young faces wreathed in smiles. My innocence showed. That was the last picture we took in college before we broke up.

"Yeah, it's the same picture just a different frame of course."

I didn't want to remember that time in my life, but the picture brought back the memories of his betrayal. Just as that picture crashed so did my heart on that awful night. Taking the picture from my hand, Drake placed it back on his desk.

"Just by the expression on your face, I know where your mind has gone. Don't go there baby, please. Let's leave the past in the past and move forward. I'm not that weak boy anymore. I'm a strong man and I will never hurt you like that again."

"Is that a promise?" I asked as I wrapped my arms around his waist and inhaled the sexy scent of his cologne.

"It is a promise as well as a fact," he said as his arms snaked around my waist.

I wanted to believe him with my whole heart. I knew he would make a great father to our child. I didn't doubt that for a minute. If I wanted it to work, I had to trust him and his love for me. Our love for each other would be enough to make it work. As I hugged him tighter, I just knew it would.

Chapter 18

I couldn't believe how relaxed and at home I felt around Drake. The only nagging thought I had was how his son was going to accept me and his new brother or sister. He assured me that little Drake knew about me and we would tell him about the baby soon. Thinking about how ecstatic Bernadette would be when I told her the news of my pregnancy, I decided to give her a call. "Hey girl, I got some news," I said before she could start talking.

"Don't keep me in suspense! I have some news of my own after you tell yours. It's about David," she added as if that would get my interest piqued.

"News about David can wait," I said. "Do you remember how I was getting nauseated and getting those migraines?"

"Yeah, I do. Are you okay?"

"Yes, it turns out I'm pregnant."

"My God Alyssa! Are you going to tell David? Will this cause problems with you and Drake?"

"Slow down. First of all, David doesn't have anything to do with my pregnancy. We used protection every time. Second of all, this baby is Drake's, who happens to be more than happy to become a father again."

"Whew! Girl, you had a sista worried there for a minute. There definitely would have been some drama if the situation had been reversed. Congratulations to you both. I am happy for you and I know without a doubt you're going to make me the Godmother."

"I wouldn't name anyone else but you," I said thinking that if Denise had been alive my baby would have two Godmothers. I knew she was bursting at the seams to tell me her news, so I said, "Tell me your news about David."

"Serena and I were out in the park yesterday. David came jogging by as we were power walking. After noticing it was me, he stopped and wanted to know where you was. He said he had been by your apartment several times and you weren't there."

"Tell me you didn't tell him where I was!"

"No! I didn't tell that cheater anything," she exclaimed. I breathed a sigh of relief as she began speaking again. "But you know what, Alyssa? That fool Serena sang like a bird! She couldn't hold water if she tried. She told him, 'you mean to tell me you didn't know your girlfriend was in Alabama.' I started to punch that fool in her mouth with a 1- 2- 3 punch like I was Layla Ali."

"Damn! Why did Serena have to open her big mouth?"

"He also said he had been calling you and his calls would go straight to voicemail."

"I have no intention of answering his calls and if you see him again you can tell him exactly how I feel."

"That's nothing but a word to me," Bernadette said. "I'll tell him to put it where the sun don't shine with pleasure. Those sexy green eyes of his didn't have me fooled one bit, Alyssa. I always felt his high polished ass could be a capital D-O-G."

"We both did wrong, Bernadette. I slept with Drake without protection, and that's why I'm in this condition now."

"Alyssa, I will tell you again. Men do that shit all the time, as you found out with David. He had an ongoing affair with that woman and you were only with Drake that one time before you broke up with David. Enough about David. I miss you like crazy, but I am happy for you. You have a second chance with your first love. How cool is that?"

"I miss you too, girl! I am also grateful for this second chance with Drake. Maybe this time we will get it right. I love him so much that it scares me sometimes."

"Are you over David entirely, Alyssa? You can be honest with me. What you say stays between us."

"I do love David," I replied honestly. "But, not with the same intensity I feel for Drake."

"That is some deep shit. Most women can't keep one man and you got two."

"Girl, you are crazy. Remember, I already broke up with David."

"You may have broken up with him, but that man still wants you."

"Well, he can want Rachael, because what we had is over." We continued to chat for a while before promising to stay in touch.

Chapter 19

Whew! After hours of shopping, with two young girls in tow, I wanted to kick off my shoes and have a long soak in the tub. Alisha and Alexis pulled me in and out of so many stores, I lost count. The stop at the food court was the only time they would sit still. While they were eating, they sat still long enough for Alisha to tell me that her sister had a crush on some little boy named Jason who was in a grade above them in school. That little information almost became a full-blown argument when Alexis denied it vehemently.

"He always pull on my hair," Alexis said.

I smiled as I took a sip from my raspberry lemonade. Their conversation really amused me. "I think he pulls your hair to get your attention Lexi, so don't be too hard on him," I said.

"You really think so Auntie?" she asked smiling.

"I know so," I said with a wink.

"See, I told you she likes him," Lisha said with pride in proving she was right all along.

Finishing lunch, I walked with the girls to Aeropostale to browse the store, while I ran across to Victoria Secrets. I could still keep my eyes on them at the same time. I wanted to purchase something sexy to surprise Drake later that evening. Spotting a fire engine red negligee with a matching thong in my size, I purchased it and went to get the girls so that I could drop them off at home.

Surprised that Drake made it home before me, I pulled behind his SUV, because a black BMW was blocking my way into the garage. Pulling my purchases from the car, I entered through the side door that lead into the kitchen. I placed my bags on the counter top and began to search for Drake. Finding him, I also found my worst nightmare – Autumn Blake Peterson – standing much too close to him for my comfort. Her Chanel #5 perfume was so loud it was overpowering and made me sick to my stomach.

When her hand reached out and touched the side of his face, it was enough to send me running up the stairs and to the bathroom where I promptly emptied the contents of my lunch into the toilet. I could hear Drake calling out to me. I flushed the toilet and rinsed my mouth with mouthwash.

"Baby, are you alright?" he asked coming up behind me and rubbing my back. Looking at him through the mirror, he had a look of concern etched in his face, but that was not all I saw.

Turning to make sure my eyes weren't playing tricks on me, I saw a smear of pink lipstick staining Drake's collar. I hoped I wasn't seeing what I thought.

"Did I interrupt anything?" I asked with attitude as I lifted his collar for a closer inspection.

"You don't ever have to ask that. This is your home just as much as it's mine and nothing is off limits to you, baby."

"Well, I guess nothing is off limits to Autumn either is there? You need to pull off that shirt, her lipstick is on your collar and it reeks of her perfume."

"Baby, calm down. Don't go jumping to any conclusions. Getting upset can't be good for our baby."

"Drake just go back to Autumn. I'm going

to take a bath and I want to be left alone!"

"She has already left. She was about to leave when you came in anyway."

"How convenient," I said with sarcasm in my voice. "Now, if you don't want me to be upset, I strongly suggest you get out of my face right now."

"Alright baby. I'm going to go and fix you some herbal tea. It should help settle your stomach. I'll bring it back up in a little bit," he said in a patient tone.

Crossing my arms across my chest, I stared him down until he got the message and left. Sinking into the bubble-filled tub, I closed my eyes and tried to get the disturbing picture of Autumn and Drake out of my head. That hussy had some nerve, I had to give her that much. If she thought I would give up and rollover like I did twelve years ago she had another thought coming. I had to trust that Drake would keep his word about not hurting me in that way again. It was Autumn that I would never trust. She was a bitch dog in heat and it looked like things would never change with her.

Trying to relax, I smoothed my hands over my stomach as I thought about the tiny life growing inside of me. Hearing a noise, I opened my eyes and looked into Drake's beautiful light hazel eyes, a trait that I hoped our baby would inherit. His wavy hair was damp from a recent shower. I thanked God I didn't have to smell her anymore. He had replaced the lipstick stained shirt with a well-worn Dallas cowboys T-shirt. Putting his hands in the water, he covered my hands with his.

"I love you and only you. I will never do anything to disrespect you or our baby. Autumn will forever be Autumn and I promise you that I will handle her. If it wasn't for the son we share, I wouldn't even give her the time of day."

"Did you kiss her?" I asked feeling the old jealousy creep into my being.

"She tried and I pushed her away. That must've been when the lipstick got on my collar. To be honest, I really don't know how it got there. Trust me baby. I know it's hard and I'm asking a lot of you, but will you do that for me?" he asked as his hand swept over my tender breasts. That one sweep of his hand ignited a fire deep inside.

"I will try," I said with a sigh. "I promise, I'll try my hardest to trust you."

I moaned as his finger slid down my stomach and slipped into my core. It wasn't long before I moved with the motion of his finger and a satisfying orgasm ripped through my body. Water sluiced over the tub wetting the tile.

"Let me help you out of the tub. I don't want you falling on the wet floor," he said.

I stood and he wrapped me in a big fluffy towel. He lifted my thickness into his strong arms without so much as a grunt. Laying me down onto the turned down bed, he dried me off, pulled the towel from my body and gazed upon it as if I was a piece of art.

"I will forever thank God for giving me another chance with you. You get more and more beautiful each day."

Reaching into his nightstand, he pulled out a familiar looking black box. I sat up on the bed as he kneeled on one knee and took out the same four-carat square cut diamond ring he tried to give me twelve years earlier. I gasped in surprise as tears glossed my eyes. He took my hand into his.

"Alyssa, I'm asking you for the second time in my life, will you marry me?"

Smiling through tears that fell freely, I said softly, "Yes, Drake. I will marry you."

I was surprised the ring fit when he placed it on my finger. "It's still beautiful," I said in awe as I admired it.

Kissing my ring finger as if to seal the deal, he pulled me to him and nuzzled my belly with the side of his face. "You smell so delicious, sweetheart. I can't get enough of your touch or the taste of you on my tongue."

"Mmmm," I moaned as he pushed me back on the bed, pulled my thighs toward him and draped my legs onto his wide shoulders. Diving in, he devoured me with the intensity of a starving man. My passion overflowed as I clutched his head between my thighs and gyrated my hips to match the storm brewing inside and threatening to erupt at any given moment.

"Drake!" The orgasm that swept through me left me limp and pliable to him as he climbed onto the bed and pumped into me. As I wrapped my legs around his waist, my passion was renewed once again.

"Hmmm, you taste so good woman. All of

this is mine," he said as he reached between our bodies and rubbed my sensitive clit. "I'm never letting you go and don't ever think about giving my pussy to anyone else."

Looking into Drake's desire-glazed eyes that held such raw emotion, the intensity of his statement made my heart beat faster. "I'm yours. I'm going to be your wife, and of course, I'll be faithful to you." I panted between my words. "But, you better be faithful to me in return or it will be over forever this time."

"That's a promise," he said as he lowered his lips to mine and kissed me as he hit my G spot. I coated his dick with my juices and he sprayed my walls with his hot seed as wave after wave of pleasure tumbled us into oblivion.

Chapter 20

The summer was flying by. I was keeping my doctor visits and my pregnancy was going smoothly. School would begin in three weeks' time. Drake wanted me to write a letter of resignation to the school board. If I renewed my contract, I would be locked in for another year. Rubbing my hand over my rounded belly, I knew I would be writing that letter of resignation. I planned to return to New York, at least long enough to take care of closing my apartment and to say goodbye to friends. I didn't want to leave the packing of my personal things to professionals.

Dr. Washington gave me the okay to fly.

Getting Drake to agree to it would be another matter altogether. With that thought, I decided to cook him a home-cooked meal that would hopefully ease him into my way of thinking. I had a couple of hours before he would be home, so I went into the kitchen to get things started. By the time he came through the door, the aroma of baked chicken, mac and cheese, collard greens, golden corn bread and a lemon-iced pound cake awaited him like it was Sunday dinner. Wrapping his arms around my waist, he nuzzled me behind my ear.

"You've made all my favorite things for dinner, Alyssa! You are a sweetheart."

"I just wanted you to know how much I love you and how much you mean to me."

"I love you and our little bundle of joy more than you will ever know. Now, give your man a kiss."

"Ask and you shall receive," I said as I laid one on him.

Sitting across from him as he worked on seconds thirty minutes later, I decided it was time for me to broach the subject of going back to New York for a couple of weeks. "You know that school starts in three weeks and I really need to go back and take care of a few things. Before you say anything, the quicker I take care of things on my end, the quicker I can come back and we can plan our wedding."

He took a sip from his tea and wiped his mouth with a cloth napkin before speaking. "Alyssa, I have no problem with you going to New York."

Breathing a sigh of relief, I couldn't believe how quick he agreed. "Good! It won't take but a couple of weeks for me to take care of my business and I'll be back before you know it."

"Sweetie, it won't take you two weeks to

take care of your business, because I'm going with you and we can knock out whatever you need to do in half that time. When are we leaving?"

"You don't have to do that. I know you are very busy here with your center."

"I have people in place to handle things when I'm away, unless you don't want me going with you for some reason," he said with a raised brow.

"Stop being silly. Of course, you are welcome to come with me. I just didn't want to keep you from the community center."

"Two weeks is too long to have you out of my sight. You're stuck with me so get used to it," he said with a gleam in his eyes. "Come here baby," he said sliding back his chair and pulling me onto his lap. "This is the best meal I have had in a long time. Thank you, baby."

"You are most welcome, kind sir. I'm glad you enjoyed it. I think we both need a good workout after a meal like this," I said.

"Baby, you just read my mind. Go on upstairs, while I take care of the dishes. I want you good and naked when I get up there. I want you in our bed wet and waiting."

After he gave me a sensuous, titillating kiss, I ran upstairs already wet and ready for my man. When he entered the bedroom minutes later, I was naked and face down, booty up on the bed.

"Damn baby! You're definitely wet for me. I can see you glistening from here," he said.

Looking over my shoulder, I gave him a come hither look and crooked my finger for him to come and take me without foreplay. I didn't need foreplay that night. I wanted him pumping into me fast and furious with animalistic pleasure.

Wasting no time, he was out of his clothes and taking me from behind leaving no doubt in my mind that he was up to the challenge of bringing us pleasure long into the night.

Chapter 21

A week later, we had no problems getting a flight to New York. Drake arranged everything, including having a car service waiting at the airport on arrival to use at our disposal. He tipped the driver and gathered our luggage. I opened door to my stuffy apartment, and Drake followed me inside.

"Welcome to my humble abode! The bedroom is through that door," I said.

"Nice place," he said coming up to me and wrapping his arms around my waist after placing the luggage in the bedroom.

Pulling his full lips to mine, I let him know without words how happy it made me to pack my home and start a life with him.

The next few days flew by. I notified the school that I would not be returning for the upcoming school year. The school board promised me a glowing recommendation if I ever needed one. I was sad and happy at the same time to leave. My emotions were running at an all-time high.

Drake was no stranger to New York and he didn't need me to play tour guide. However, I did take him to one of my favorite places in the world. The Botanic Gardens in Brooklyn was beautiful that time of the year. We walked around for hours until our stomachs began to growl. Finding a nearby restaurant was the easy part as they had several to choose from.

"Baby what's your pleasure?" Drake asked.

"Let's go to Louie's Pizzeria. Their pizza is

wonderful day Drake and I just shared. I could feel the short hairs on the back of my neck rise and I knew David's eyes were boring into my back.

"Before the pizza comes, I need to visit the ladies room. I'll be right back," I said.

Standing as I stood, Drake pulled me to him and placed a soft kiss on my lips leaving no doubt that I belonged to him and him alone.

As I passed David's table, I made sure to avoid all eye contact. The restrooms were set off in a dimly lit part of the restaurant with the women and men rooms directly across from one another. I was opening the door to enter the restroom when I heard my name called softly. I hurried into the restroom, but before I could shut the door and click the lock David pushed his way in behind me.

"Get out!" I shouted. "You can't be in here."

I just want to talk to you, Alyssa. Why haven't you returned any of my calls? We meant too much to each other for you to treat me in this way!"

"Treat you like what, David? We're not together anymore and as you can see I've moved on and it seems as if you have too. Is that reason enough for not returning your calls?"

Ignoring my question, he said, "My God, you look so beautiful! You are practically glowing."

Nervous, my hand went protectively to my stomach. His eyes followed my hands and saw the rounded evidence of my pregnancy. Looking at me with his accusing green eyes, he asked, "Why didn't you call and tell me that you were pregnant? When were you going to tell me that I was going to be a father? I will not let you run across the country with some other man raising my child. There is no way in hell that I will stand for that!"

"David! Please, calm down," I said wanting him to lower his voice. "This baby is not yours, it's Drakes. I promise you I will explain, but this is not the time or the place," I said trying to calm the anger that was seething from his pores.

"Damn it! You will explain things now or I won't be responsible for what happens next."

"David, are you threatening me?" I was trying to remain calm, but he was beginning to work a nerve. "You realize we used protection whenever we had sex right? There is no way that this baby can be yours. I am 110% positive that this baby is Drake's."

"That can mean only one thing. You had sex with him when you went home to your friend's funeral. The hell you gave me and you did the same damn thing – and before I did! How hypocritical can you get?" he asked clenching his hands as he spoke. I had never witnessed David with that kind of rage before. "Fuck you, Alyssa! How could you give my pussy away?"

Feeling the anger in me rise, as a response to his cruel words, made me lash out with enough venom to hurt him. "At least you didn't walk in on me screwing in my place of business, David!"

I immediately regretted my awful words. "Listen to me David," I said in a more placating tone. "When I went home to Denise's funeral, a lot of unresolved emotions arose. I was wrong for not telling you about my part that lead to this break up. I didn't plan on being with Drake, it just happened. I came back home intending to keep my distance and not letting anything like that ever happen again with Drake.

"Oh, now it is clear. You took one look at your old college boyfriend, the same one that hurt you so bad you almost didn't give another man a chance until you met me, and you just fell into bed with him."

"We both did wrong and both of us were hurt by our actions. I never meant to intentionally hurt you. I'm happy with Drake and I hope you're happy with Rachael," I said as I pushed a stray wisp of my hair behind my ear. Catching a flash of my engagement ring, David took my hand and looked at it with a sneer on his lips.

"Are you engaged now?"

"As a matter of fact, I am."

"How could you fall out of love with me so fast? I still love you, Alyssa. I love you so much that it hurts," he said dropping my ring finger as if it was too hot to the touch.

I didn't want Drake to come looking for me, so I said, "David let me out or Drake will think something is wrong."

When I attempted to step around him, he pushed me back against the wall and kissed me like a man fighting for his life. Trying to twist my face away was unsuccessful. He held my face in a vise like grip and thrust his tongue into my mouth. David was a great kisser and, even in his anger, deep rooted feelings resurfaced that left me wondering how I could still catch feelings from his kiss when the man I was going to marry was somewhere outside that door.

God help me! I thought. I was completely disgusted with myself. Finding the strength to resist, I pushed David away from me and tears formed in my eyes.

"David, please let me go. If you still love me like you say you do, you will leave me alone."

"That's the problem. I love you so much I don't know if I can let you go that easy. It doesn't matter that you may be pregnant with another man's child," he said touching my stomach. For the first time in my pregnancy, I felt a flutter as his hand settled on my stomach. Smiling, he felt it too. "I will make a good father to your baby. Just give me another chance, please. I know you still feel something for me. I felt it in our kiss."

"Wait a minute, David. You kissed me, remember. I didn't want nor ask for it," I said in total denial of how much the kiss affected me.

"True, but it didn't stop you from enjoying it," he said.

"Go back to Rachael." I removed his hand from my stomach. When I tried to leave that time, he opened the door for me and let me go with a defeated look in his eyes.

Chapter 22

"Baby, I was just getting ready to look for you. What's wrong?" Drake asked noticing my red eyes.

"Can we take this pizza to go?" I asked noticing the steaming pizza on the table.

"Sure babe," he said as he signaled the waitress who was more than happy to box our pizza to go. Drake left a generous tip and we left the restaurant, but not before noticing that Rachael no longer occupied the booth she sat in earlier.

"Are you ready to tell me what happened in

the restaurant that caused you to want to leave?" Drake asked as we were getting ready for bed.

"David confronted me and we had words. To make a long story short, I made it crystal clear that I don't ever want to see or hear from him again."

"Maybe it's time for me to have a talk with this guy. I don't think he'll be giving up as easy as you think he will. I know that I wouldn't if I was in his shoes."

"Let it go, Drake. He knows that we are engaged and I'm having your baby. You are the one that I love and nothing will ever change that."

"You look tired, baby. Come here," Drake said pulling me close and wrapping his muscular arms around me.

Feeling a sense of peace and comfort, I closed my eyes and fell into a deep sleep, hoping David would leave well enough alone and the words I had spoken to Drake would not become a lie.

***

Finally, I was able to introduce Bernadette to Drake. "I've heard nothing but good things about you Bernadette," Drake told her.

"I've heard all about you, too," she said extending her hand. "All I'm going to say is Alyssa is like a sister to me and if you ever hurt her again there will be hell to pay."

"I'll remember that," Drake said looking over at me with a smile. I warned him about Bernadette's mouth and how she didn't mince her words. "You don't ever have to worry about me hurting her again. I learned my lesson of a lifetime when she walked out my life twelve years ago. I will not give her reason to ever walk away from me again."

"Why are the two of you talking as if I'm not in the room?" I asked.

Softening her tone, Bernadette looked at me with misty eyes. "You know I'm going to miss the hell of you right?"

"No more than I will miss you," I replied with a quiver in my voice. "We can always visit each other and you can come down south to complain how hot it is in the summers and complain about the mosquitoes. Some of them are that big girl," I said stretching my hands far apart in exaggeration.

We all laughed lightening the mood and the conversation went much smoother after that. I was glad when Drake suggested giving us two friends time alone, so we could catch up. Once he closed the door behind him, I turned to Bernadette and said, "I got news for you!"

Patting the space on the sofa for me to sit,

she said, "Well, spill it. Don't keep me in suspense."

"Drake and I saw David and his girlfriend at a restaurant yesterday," I said cutting to the chase. "When I went to the restroom, David's ass had the nerve to follow me in the ladies room and the audacity to lock the door."

"I know that fool is crazy now," Bernadette laughed. "Did he try to talk his way back into your life?"

"You know he did and I made it clear how I feel about Drake. I think he finally got the message that we are over."

"How did he handle it, Alyssa?"

"Not very well, I'm afraid. He said how much he loved me, even going as far as saying that he would raise the baby as his own when he found that I was pregnant."

"What did I tell you before? You have two men who love you and some of us can't even find a piece of a man. Umph! Umph! Umph!"

"Bernadette, you need to cut that mess out." I couldn't help but to laugh at her silliness.

"I have a feeling that you left something out. What else happened between you two?"

Looking down at the carpet, I softly muttered, "He kissed me."

"I knew it!" She exclaimed. "What did Drake do when you told him?"

"What do you mean what did Drake do? Are you crazy?"

"Yeah, you're right. It might not be the best idea to tell him something like that. I might have been hearing about David on the 6 o'clock news." She giggled. "I can see the headlines

247

now. Bank executive beat to a pulp by ex-pro football player, Drake Peterson, former defensive lineman for the Dallas Cowboys." Clutching her mid-section, she fell into uncontrollable laughter and I couldn't help but to join in. That was what I loved about that woman. She could turn a grave situation into something hilarious every time.

"Girl you know I'm going to miss your crazy butt right?"

"Like you said earlier, we will visit and we definitely will keep in touch. That's a promise. We may not be sisters by blood, but we are most definitely sisters by bond and don't you forget that," she said.

Chapter 23

Two weeks passed since I closed my apartment and moved my things that were shipped from New York. The bigger items I gave away and some I left behind for the next tenant that lived there. Over dinner, Drake wanted to talk about the kind of wedding I wanted.

"Don't take this the wrong way, but I rather have something small. I'm sporting a baby bump and I don't want a big wedding or anything fancy."

"Baby, we are two grown adults. We don't have to please anyone but ourselves. If it's a small wedding you want that is what we will have."

"Thanks baby," I said. "I was thinking we could invite your family, Bernadette, Weston and the girls. Oh, and of course, I know you will want Drake Jr. to come."

"That sounds good to me sweetheart and speaking of Junior, I wanted to talk to you about him."

"I'm listening," I said as I gave him my full attention.

"I really want you to know my son and him to get to know you. I was thinking since his school doesn't start until September, he could come here his last two weeks before school starts."

"Sure Drake, I don't have a problem with that at all. How will Autumn feel about that? I know she doesn't like me and the feeling is mutual on my end."

"Autumn won't have a say in this. He's my son, too. Whether she agrees to it or not is a moot point. I have visiting rights and there's nothing that she can do about that."

A week later, I nervously awaited Drake to come from the airport with his son. I didn't know how he would accept me or what things Autumn had told him about me. However, I fixed a simple kid friendly dinner in hopes that it would be a start for him to form his own opinion of me. Hearing the garage door open, I knew they had arrived. Taking off my apron, I hurried into the family room and picked up a magazine, so I would appear relaxed.

"Hey baby, we're home," Drake called out. "Where are you?"

"I'm in the family room," I answered and stood as they appeared in the doorway. Smiling, I approached the pair with butterflies dancing in my stomach.

"Junior, this is Alyssa, the woman I was telling you about. The woman that I'm going to marry and the mother of your soon to be baby brother or sister."

Drake Jr. was tall for an eleven year old with a head full of curly hair and hazel eyes. He was a little heartbreaker in the making, just like his dad.

"Hi, Miss Alyssa," he said as he extended his hand for me to shake like a true little gentleman. He looked so much like his dad; it was like looking at a replica of Drake. His light brown coloring was the only resemblance of his mother.

"I think I can do a little better than a handshake," I said as I opened my arms. He didn't hesitate to step into my embrace and give me a warm hug in return. Looking at Drake, I found a warm smile on his face and a loving look in his eyes that told me everything

252

would be just fine with our joining family.

"What's that smelling so good?" Drake Jr. asked with the look of a growing boy with a good appetite.

"Go with your dad and put your luggage in your room. By the time you come back down everything will be on the table."

"Cool," he said, dashing out the door and up the stairs with his backpack leaving Drake to follow with his shoulder bag.

"Thanks baby," Drake said as he looked back at me and then retraced his steps to kiss me fully on my lips before dashing up the stairs behind his son.

Drake's son proved to be talkative and informative, while eating breakfast the next morning. "Did dad tell you he named his community centers after you and him?" he asked while stuffing his face with blueberry waffles.

Looking at Drake in surprise, I was at a loss for words. I stuttered, "No... No, he didn't. I always assumed the A stood for your mom's name."

"Finish your breakfast Jr.," instructed Drake. "I meant to tell you but never found the right time to tell you. We'll talk about it later if you don't mind?" Drake looked at me with a questioning look in his eyes.

"Of course, I don't mind," I answered with tears glossing my eyes. Anything and everything seemed to make me more sentimental those days.

Chapter 24

"Hey Wes! What are you and the girls doing on Labor Day weekend?" I asked over the phone.

"We have no concrete plans. What's up?"

"I was wondering if you could come over for a little cookout. It will just be you and the girls and us. Drake wants to do a little something before Drake Jr. leaves."

"We will be there. What can I bring?" Weston asked.

"Just bring yourself. Come Saturday any time after three or better yet come early and I'll put the girls to work helping me peel the potatoes for my potato salad."

"You got it! We will see you then."

Hanging up my call with Wes, my phone

instantly began to ring again. Thinking Weston had forgotten something, I answered without checking the caller I.D.

"Alyssa, I really need to see you," David's voice slurred.

"Why are you calling me? And, are you drunk this early in the day?" I couldn't help but to ask.

"I need to see you. I know I can fix us if you give me another chance," he begged.

"David, please! Don't call me again. If you force me, I will have my number changed." Not waiting for a response I ended the call quite disturbed.

Saturday was a beautiful day and full of sunshine. A great day for a cookout. Drake looked so sexy in his Southpole shorts and shirt. His long feet were encased in brown leather sandals.

"Am I peeling the potatoes right?" Alisha asked drawing my attention away from the window where I was watching Drake man the grill. I would never get tired of looking at that man.

"Yes, you are! You're doing an excellent job and so are you Alexis. You two are the greatest little helpers. Thank you!"

"Auntie Alyssa, we love helping you and when the baby comes we can babysit," Alexis said.

"We'll see," I said smiling. "Let's see if you two feel that way once the baby gets here. After all the dirty diapers you may have a change of heart."

"Alexis can change the diapers and I'll give the baby the bottle," Alisha said.

"Why do I have to change dirty diapers?"

Alexis demanded. "I want to feed the baby and you can do the diapers," she said pouting.

"Girls," I said intervening. "Let's concentrate on getting the potato salad made and when my baby arrives I will show you both how to feed him or her."

"Okay," they readily agreed.

After all of my side dishes were made, we went out to the patio and joined the guys. Wrapping my arms around Drake as he flipped the burgers, I laid my head on his back and relished the feel of his tight muscles through his shirt. I didn't know what had gotten into me lately, but I wanted him so much. Just the thought of Drake making love to me was enough to saturate my panties.

"Baby, if you keep rubbing me like that, I'm going to forget about our guests and take you upstairs."

Weston cleared his throat and I looked over

to where he was sitting with the girls and Drake Jr. who were watching us with rapt interest.

"Oh, sorry," I said with an embarrassed blush to my cheeks.

Turning and whispering in my ear, Drake said, "Don't be sorry. Just know that I'll be taking care of all your needs tonight." Turning me and pushing me toward the table, he swatted me playfully on my hips. "Now, go sit with everyone else so that I can finish up without burning the food."

Weston shook his head as I sat beside him. "I would've never dreamed you and Drake would find your way back to each other or that you would be getting married and having his child. Denise would've been proud, just as I am."

Thinking of Denise brought bittersweet joy to my face. "You are right, Wes. Denise was always Drake and my biggest advocate. I'm very blessed. I already love Drake Jr. and this baby will make our family complete."

Later that night after the food was put away, dishes washed and Drake Jr. sound asleep, Drake kept his promise and made delicious love to me. Starting at my freshly pedicured feet, he took every single toe into his mouth. Kissing his way slowly from my feet to my inner thighs where he bit the fleshy part of my thigh, leaving his mark as he honed in on my sweet honey pot. He worshipped me with relish that had me grabbing the pillows to cover my face as a scream escaped my lips from the intense pleasure. In that moment in time, I knew without a doubt that there would never be another man that could please and love me like Drake. Making love to him was never just about sex. It was an experience where each part of me was an active participant. My heart, body and soul.

Him saying, "Come for me, baby," was all it

took for me to come apart and released my juices into his beautiful mouth. He received them as if it was nectar from the gods. My release was so sweet that tears seeped from my eyes as he gathered me into his arms and entered me with bare restraint as he pumped into me. I bit my lip as passion once again began to stir. He hit my G spot time and time again. My muscles tightened around him and milked his love so good that he called my name as he came with me, riding out our orgasm as one.

Chapter 25

I said my goodbyes to Drake Jr. knowing that he would be back the following month for our wedding. A very small wedding it would be. I hoped Bernadette would be able to make it. Drake's parents, his younger sister, Sharne', Weston and the girls would be there.

Sometimes, I regretted being an only child. Having no close family made me sad on occasions such as this. Marrying Drake meant more to me than gaining a husband or a father for my child. His family would become my very own. For that, I was more than grateful.

October was cooler than usual for the

south. My wedding day was fast approaching and my pregnancy was more obvious by the day. October 23rd was the day of my wedding and it was only three weeks away. I was almost six months into my pregnancy and enjoying every minute of it, especially since my morning sickness had long passed. Drake pampered me so much that I was becoming spoiled.

Picking up my cell, I speed dialed Bernadette. I knew she would be on her lunch break by then. "Hey girl! What's up?" She asked as her usual greeting.

"I'm just making sure you will be here in three weeks for my wedding."

"I'm already there, so don't worry about a thing, sweetie. I just don't want to hear any excuses about our girls' night out when I get there," Bernadette stated.

"I won't give you any static woman," I said laughing. "You do realize I'm almost six months pregnant, though? There is only so much partying that I can do."

"Alyssa, you are even more beautiful pregnant. Don't you dare let this pregnancy stop you from letting your hair down once in awhile? We will have a good time when I come, so get ready," she said.

"You won't get any argument from me. By the way, Drake has already arranged your ticket at the airport. A car service has been arranged to pick you up once you get to ATL to bring you here on the 20th."

"Girl, shut your mouth! Drake shouldn't have went all out for me like that, but I'm not going to complain. I feel like royalty." She giggled.

"It was no problem. He was more than happy to do it. He knows how happy it will make me to have you here. Besides Denise, I couldn't ask for a better sister."

"Now, you're going to make me cry and

mess up my makeup. Good thing my lunch break is almost over and I really have to go. I love you, Alyssa," she said before ending the call.

A few days later, I was telling Drake, "I'll be fine, I promise. Go and handle your business, Bernadette will be arriving tomorrow. Then, your parents and sister will be arriving the day after that from Florida."

"Baby, I know. I just hate having to go on a business trip this close to our wedding. I also don't want to miss your doctor's appointment scheduled for later today."

"You are a sweetheart. You have been to all my appointments with me, missing one isn't going to hurt. I'd rather you take care of your business now so that our wedding day won't have any interruptions."

"Alright, give me a kiss woman. The sooner I leave, the sooner I get back."

Wrapping my arms around his neck, I pulled him into a hot kiss that would have him thinking about me long after he was gone. I relished the exotic smell of his cologne and the feel of his tongue as it dueled with mine making heat rise in me with his every look and touch. Moaning, I could feel him hardening against me. Knowing that he didn't have much time, I pushed him into a sitting position on the bed. Kneeling before him, I unzipped his pants and reached inside of his briefs.

"Wait Alyssa, you don't..."

Not letting him finish his sentence, I took him into my mouth. Feeling him hit the back of my throat, I relaxed my throat to accommodate as much of him as I could. Running his hands through my hair, he massaged my scalp as I closed my eyes and gave myself over to pleasing him. I loved the feel, taste and texture of him. Pulling back to the tip, I licked and sucked around his sensitive head, loving the taste of his precum. It was true about certain nectars and juices making your secretion sweet, because Drake was so sweet and good that I enveloped him and sucked until he came in my mouth with a rush. He moaned over and over as I swallowed every last drop.

Pulling out of my mouth with a pop, he was breathing as if he had just run a marathon. The smile on his face was all the satisfaction I needed. The smile also held retribution. He pulled me onto the bed and gave me the same loving that I had just bestowed on him.

Later that evening after leaving the doctor's office, I really hated to go home to an empty house. I was missing Drake already and he had only been gone a couple of hours. Not wanting to cook, I grabbed a salad on my way home and stopped at the Movie Warehouse to pick up a few DVD's to keep me company.

Chapter 26

Bernadette arrived around noon and I was ecstatic to see her. "It's about time you got here girl," I said hugging her as if it had been years since we saw each other instead of almost two months.

Stepping back from my embrace, she said, "Let me look at you. Girl, you are in full bloom now. Pregnancy becomes you. Just look how much you glow! I know your secret though," Bernadette continued to chatter.

"What's my secret?" I asked taking the bait, knowing I was being setup.

"Pregnancy isn't the only thing that got you glowing. Getting good dick on the regular will do that that to you too," she said with a cackle.

I couldn't stop myself. I laughed so hard that I had to stop and catch a breath. "I will say it again. Bernadette you are one crazy woman, but I love you to death. When Drake's family gets here, you better put a muzzle on that mouth of yours!"

"Child, please! I know how to act. I teach a bunch of knuckleheads every day. Remember?"
"Now, that's what I'm talking about. You know you ain't right for calling those kids knuckleheads."

Rolling her eyes in exaggeration, she said, "You know I'm only teasing. Now, come on and show me this beautiful house of yours. This place puts my little apartment to shame," she added looking around.

"Who you talking to? My apartment was

the same size as yours. It put mines to shame too and I must admit I'm enjoying living here much better."

"Lyssa, the driver wouldn't even accept the tip I tried to give him. He said that Mr. Peterson had taken care of everything. Your man must be loaded!"

"I don't know about all of that, but I do know he's able to give back to the community in a big way. That's one of the reasons I love him so much. He is so giving."

"I'm so happy for you! Getting a second chance with Drake is just beautiful," she said.

"I know, believe me when I say I count my blessings every day. But enough about us, I know you're probably hungry. Let me show you to your room first, so you can put your things up. Just come on back down to the kitchen when you're ready."

270

"You don't have to ask me twice. You know I'm ready to get my grub on."

Leaving her in her room to unpack, I went into the kitchen to get our lunch ready. Minutes later, we were enjoying a healthy lunch.

"This chicken salad is the bomb," she said taking another sandwich from the plate. You always did know your way around a kitchen."

"Yeah I do, but I had to start making healthier choices," I said rubbing my stomach. With this little one on the way, I had too.

Reaching over and touching my belly, she said, "I can't wait 'til you get here. I am going to be the best Godmother ever!" After a while of silence, Bernadette looked at me as if she had something bothersome on her mind. "Alyssa, I didn't want to bring this up, but I saw David before I left and that brotha wasn't himself at all. I don't know what you were putting on that man when you were together but, whatever it was, you left him in a bad way."

"I'm surprised at you, of all people. You're acting like you feel sorry for the guy. Whatever happened to your hard stance on cheating men and screw them before they screw you philosophy?"

"I know girl but, if you had seen him, you would have felt sorry for him too."

"My wedding is in two days and I do not want to spend this time talking about the woes of David. Do you understand?"

"Sorry Lyssa. From now on, my lips are sealed. No more David talk."

"Thank you," I said with a wave of my hand. David's mess would only add confusion to the beautiful blessings going on in my life.

On a lighter note, I couldn't wait for

Bernadette and Weston to meet. I so wanted my two best friends to get along. Besides that, they both were just like family. Weston was meeting us at the Auburn Supper Club at nine. I was dressed in black maternity tights and a long yellow and silver tunic. I paired it with my silver flats, because I didn't want to be dealing with swollen feet the next day. Bernadette was ready and waiting for me downstairs. She wore a fitted black and gray sweater dress with heeled boots.

"Mama, you are looking good," she said as I stepped into the room.

"You don't look too bad yourself," I said as she twirled with her hands on her hips. "Let's go," I said grabbing my purse and keys as we walked out the door.

We paid our ten-dollar cover charge as we entered the Auburn Supper club. Spotting Weston almost instantly, I told Bernadette to follow me to a back corner table where he was sitting. He watched us as we made our way towards him.

Bernadette whispered, "Girl! Is that your friend you was telling me about?"

"Yeah, and you better be on your best behavior," I said as if she was two instead of thirty two. "And he's off limits. He's still grieving, so don't push!"

"What?" She said like she was innocent. "I could offer him solace on my breasts... Ah, I meant to say shoulders. You know how I do," she added with a wink.

"Exactly lady! So hands off," I reiterated as we arrived at his table.

"Hey sweetie." He rose and kissed my cheek as he stood for us to be seated. "You are looking gorgeous tonight, but that's nothing new," he complimented.

"Thank you, Wes. You're looking mighty

handsome yourself," I returned with a smile. Bernadette cleared her throat to bring attention to herself. "Oh! Weston this is my friend, Bernadette, who I told you about. Bernadette this is Weston Kingsly."

"It's an honor to finally meet you, Bernadette. Alyssa speaks very highly of you," he said engulfing her hand into his much larger one. "Any friend of Lyssa's is already a friend of mine."

Showing all of her perfect, white teeth, that was the first time I saw her at a loss for words. Hitting her with my elbow, I prompted her out of her stupor so she would reply. "Nice... nice to meet you, Weston," she said with a light giggle.

Rolling my eyes, I took a seat and slid over in the booth so she could sit down beside me. Instead, she slid her big butt beside Weston into the booth he occupied earlier. She had the audacity to pat the seat, so he didn't have a choice but to sit down beside her.

"Will Drake still make it back home tomorrow?" Wes asked once seated.

"I talked to him earlier today and he's stopping to pick up Drake Jr. They should be arriving tomorrow evening. His parents will also be arriving sometime tomorrow."

"I understand that you'll be standing up for Drake," Bernadette said never taking her eyes off Weston, not even for a second.

"Yes and you'll be Lyssa's matron of honor, right?" He asked giving her his full attention.

"Maid of honor," she corrected. "I'm single."

"Who want drinks? I think I want one of those Virgin Daiquiris with extra strawberries and whip cream on top," I said interrupting their exchange.

Being the gentlemen he was, Weston ordered drinks for us all and threw in an order of wings and veggies with ranch dressing on the side. My friend knew me so well. I loved the wings there.

Sitting back listening to the soothing jazz, I looked across the table at Bernadette as she sipped on her Apple Martini. I hoped she wouldn't have too many, although it didn't too much matter since I was the one driving. Almost feeling like a third wheel, I giggled to myself as she plastered herself to Weston's side. Poor thing, he was pulling at his collar as if he was getting nervous. It was actually quite entertaining.

"Alyssa, why are you so quiet over there?" Weston asked.

"I'm just thinking about how happy I'll be to become Mrs. Drake Peterson," I said instead of telling him I was enjoying Bernadette's attempt to work her magic on him.

"I'll be glad when you're his wife, too," Weston said. "I know Denise will be looking down on your wedding day and be just as happy for you as I am."

As if on cue, Bernadette saw her chance to rub his back and tell him how sorry she was for his loss. Being an unassuming man, he fell right into her trap and lapped up the sympathy she portrayed to get close to him. *Well, another one bites the dust,* I said to myself.

Chapter 27

My wedding day had finally arrived. With my pregnancy in such an advanced state, I opted for a two-piece cream suit with a matching camisole to match. Drake was standing handsome and tall in a tailored black tux. Under a bright cloudless sky, Drake and I declared our love and faithfulness to one another in front of God. The minister who performed the simple ceremony with our friends and Drake's family made it complete.

The catered reception was a small, but happy, affair. The champagne flowed, although all I had was sparkling grape juice. When it came time to cut our three-tiered wedding cake, I did what was expected and smashed it in Drake's face as the photographer clicked away.

Bernadette had to leave right after the reception. However, she didn't leave without making sure Weston had her number in more ways than one.

Drake's parents stayed the night and kept Drake Jr. with them. The next day, they would be leaving and making sure that Drake Jr. caught his plane and his mother would be waiting for him at the airport when he landed.

I wanted to wait until after the baby came to take a real honeymoon. But, Drake went all out and booked the Honeymoon Suite at the Hilton. Looking into his eyes as he undressed me, he took his time as if he were unwrapping a fragile gift.

"Baby, I have been wanting to do this all

day. It took everything in me to keep my hands to myself," he said in a gruff voice as he kneeled in front of me. His hands wandered up my thighs to remove my cream lace panties. Taking the panties, he brought them to his nose to inhale the fragrance and moaned before sliding them into pocket of his slacks. Standing, he turned my back to him and unsnapped my matching lace bra and my heavy breasts spilled into his hands. Pressing my ass against his hardening crotch, I moaned as his hands swept across my sensitive breasts. He swept his hand further down my swollen belly. In that moment, the baby kicked hard as if to say 'don't forget about me.'

Sitting me on the bed, Drake knelt between my thighs and peppered kisses all over my stomach, softly talking to our baby as chills went throughout my body. My heart was filled with so much love for that man and our baby that I felt as if it would burst. Urging me to lay down, he trailed kisses down my thighs before opening my lips to sweep his tongue over my saturated clit. Draping one leg over his shoulder, he swept his tongue from my clit and dipped his tongue into me until I gushed against his mouth with my release. Helping me onto my knees, Drake entered me tenderly from the back and continued to love me with such tenderness until we both fell over the cliff of ecstasy together.

Chapter 28

I loved Drake more and more with each passing day. I was looking forward to the birth of our baby. The nursery had been done in neutral colors, since we didn't want to know the sex of the baby. We had even bought little sleepers that either a boy or girl could wear. Bernadette would be giving me a baby shower after my baby arrived. I could not ask for anything more from the people I loved.

Drake and I had been married for a whole month before trouble in the form of his ex-wife, Autumn, knocked on our door via UPS mail. I was well into my seventh month with swollen feet and feeling as unattractive as a whale on two feet. He was doing some paperwork at his office at the community center and would be home so we could have dinner together later that evening.

I was into the second half of Maury when the doorbell interrupted my show. I didn't need to be watching all that baby mama drama anyway, so I clicked off the television and went to answer the door. A UPS man was on the other side of the door with a shirt-sized box that I signed for and then noticed that it was from Autumn, but addressed to both Drake and myself. I thanked him and closed the door.

Surprised that Autumn had sent us a late wedding gift, I took the box upstairs with me and laid it down, deciding to open it with Drake when he got home. After taking a leisurely bath, I went downstairs to warm up the casserole I made earlier. I was just taking fresh rolls out of the oven when Drake came into the door.

"Hey baby," he said coming up to give me a hug and kiss showing me that he missed me as much as I had missed him. "How was your day?" he asked.

"It was fine Drake. I just wish that I wouldn't stay so sleepy all the time."

"Well, you better sleep now. Once the baby gets here, we won't be getting much of that," he said smiling as if he was anticipating many sleepless nights.

Later that night as we were getting ready for bed, I looked over and remembered the package from Autumn. I could hear Drake cutting off the shower as I settled into bed. Freshly showered and shaved wearing his PJ's low on his hips, he walked toward me with lust in his eyes. There I was feeling as big as a whale and he still desired me and proved it all the time. Climbing into bed, he noticed the box that was in my hands. "What's that?" He asked.

"It's from Autumn and it's addressed to the both of us. Shall I do the honors or do you want to open it?"

"By all means, you open it," he said with disinterest.

As I opened the box, I noticed a pair of black silk boxer shorts lay nestled inside, along with a note. Picking up the note, I began to read aloud.

"Drake you left your underwear when you stayed the night last month. I know how you love your silk boxers, so I had them laundered and wanted to return them in case you missed them. Oh, by the way, congratulations on your wedding nuptials. I should send a card. Until next time... Always yours, Autumn." Looking at Drake with fire in my eyes, I asked, "What is the meaning of this?"

I dumped the box and note onto his lap.

Tears were already gathering in my eyes. My nails were biting into my palms. I knew if I let my hands relax they would be slapping the shit out of Drake's handsome face. "How dare you!" I sputtered not giving him time to answer. "You promised me that I wouldn't have to go through this with you again!"

"Calm down, baby. I can explain, so don't be getting worked up over nothing."

"Nothing! You call that nothing?" I said as I pointed a finger at his underwear. "Your underwear coming back in a gift box from another woman's house is nothing?" I attempted to get out of the bed, but my baby weight made it difficult to move.

"Alyssa, listen to me," he said as he held me to him not allowing me to leave the bed. "Stop struggling please. I love you and I wouldn't do anything to mess that up." Smoothing my loose hair back from my face, he looked into my eyes.

"I'm listening," I finally calmed down enough to say. "But, you had better have a good explanation, because I won't be responsible for my actions if you don't. That much I can promise you," I said meaning every word.

"Baby, I did stay the night when I went to pick up Drake Jr. for the wedding last month. I slept on the couch. I didn't think it made sense to get a hotel room for only a couple of hours before it was time for us to catch a flight home. I decided that we could make better time if I stayed and Drake Jr. and I could catch our early flight. That is the truth, no matter what Autumn tries to insinuate in that note! She is up to her old tricks again. Please, don't let her cause trouble between us."

Autumn and her trouble-causing ways, I thought as I looked into his eyes and saw the truth of his words. She couldn't stop us from getting married, but she sure was going to try to stop us from being happy.

"If I wasn't pregnant I would go to Texas and put an old fashion whooping on her that she wouldn't soon forget. Drake, do you know, pregnant or not, you came this close to getting slugged?"

"Remind me not to cross you in the future," he said taking the box. He got up and threw it boxers and all into the trash. Now, let's start this night back over," he said pulling me into his arms with my back nestled against his chest. Wrapping his strong arms around me and the baby, he rubbed my stomach promising his undying love and devotion to our family as long as he lived.

Two months later, the fiasco Autumn tried to pull seemed like child's play compared to the labor pains rolling through my stomach. Drake was on one side holding my hand while Bernadette was on the other. She had flown in three days earlier for my original due date. I was two days past my due date when my water broke unexpectedly at the dinner table. Chaos ensued as Drake rushed me to the hospital and Bernadette screamed for him to get us there in one piece as he ran every red light on the way.

Dr. Washington explained that first babies had their own timeline of coming sometimes. She assured us not to worry. After twenty three and a half hours of grueling labor, I called Drake every name in the book and he took it in stride, although he did look a little faint when the baby's head crowned. Finally, Drayden Justin Peterson, 9 pound 2 ounces, came into the world with strong lungs making his presence felt. He was healthy and we were happy.

"Baby, we did it!" Drake shouted with all the pride of a proud father. I tried to get another look of my baby as the nurse cleaned him.

"I'm so proud of you girl," Bernadette said squeezing my hands. "He is so beautiful," she said glancing back at the baby who had quieted down.

Smiling, I was so tired. All I wanted to do was hold my son in my arms.

"Mr. Peterson, would you like to take the baby to your wife?" the doctor asked.

"Of course, I would." Drake needed no further urging as he took the baby and brought him to me gently placing him into my arms. On pulling the blanket back, I counted ten perfect toes and ten fingers. I looked into his tiny pale face hoping he would open his eyes and praying he would have his daddy's light hazel eyes.

"He must be as tired as I am," I said with a laugh. My laughter must have startled Drayden for in that moment he let out a startled cry and opened his eyes.

Looking into my baby's eyes for the first

time, he stared back at me and I covered my mouth to hold back a startled cry of my own. My baby's clear green eyes, the eyes of his daddy, were staring back at me. The eyes of a man that I never wanted to be a part of my life again.

Looking up at Drake staring down at us, I saw the sadness in his eyes. I knew he knew without a doubt that he was not our baby's father. Our baby had the eyes of his father all right, for there would be no denying that David McRay was my baby's father.

THE END

Hope you enjoyed the book!

Please return to Amazon and leave a review.

She will be republishing part 2 soon!

Other Kindle Titles By Theresa Hodge:

ASK ME AGAIN

Loving Hart

Falling For A Star

Trinity Black

The Babysitter

The Edge Of Winter

Hot Miami Knights

Nicholas North

Noelle's Rock

Noelle's Rock 2

Noelle's Rock 3

Noelle's Rock 4

Noelle's Rock 5

More of her titles can be found on Amazon

Made in the USA
Middletown, DE
04 October 2017